MUPPETS MEET THE CLASSICS

THE PHANTOM OF THE OPERA

GASTON LEROUX AND ERIK FORREST JACKSON

ILLUSTRATED BY OWEN RICHARDSON

Penguin Workshop
An Imprint of Penguin Random House

With love and gratitude to Frank and Mary Nell,
who taught me to appreciate great stories and
terrible puns in equal measure—EFJ

For my darlings, Madeline, Ozma, and Amy.
Happy is the man whom the muses love . . .
—OR

PENGUIN WORKSHOP
Penguin Young Readers Group
An Imprint of Penguin Random House LLC

Emojis © Pingebat/iStock/Thinkstock

Copyright © 2017 by Disney/Muppets. All rights reserved. Published by
Penguin Workshop, an imprint of Penguin Random House LLC, 345 Hudson Street,
New York, New York 10014. PENGUIN and PENGUIN WORKSHOP
are trademarks of Penguin Books Ltd, and the W colophon is a trademark of
Penguin Random House LLC. Printed in the USA.

Library of Congress Cataloging-in-Publication Data is available.

ISBN 9780451534378   10 9 8 7 6 5 4 3 2 1

Masked, I advance.
—René Descartes

I've fallen and I can't get up.
—The Paris Opera House Chandelier

TABLE OF CONTENTS

Chapter I

A GHOST? LIKE, *SERIOUSLY*?!

The terror had been steadily building for weeks. But that chilly January evening marked the turning point no one had anticipated.

Of course, you are no doubt here for the now-legendary tale of a particular pig and her fearless frog. Rest assured, it's a tale you'll get in full. But as with all stage-worthy dramas presented inside the fabled Paris Opera House, it's traditional to have a brief bit of scene setting in order to build anticipation for the leading players to step into the spotlight.

I must confess that while I'm not exactly traditional, I am indeed a sucker for a soupçon of suspense.

So it was on that night, just days after the start of the new year, Monsieur J.P. Grosse was throwing a final gala performance to celebrate his retirement. The gruff impresario, with his plump, pear-shaped head and caterpillar mustache, had been for the last thirty years the manager of the Opera House.[1] But Grosse said that putting up with the fragile egos of the renowned institution's persnickety performers was "durn near exhausting" and he'd had enough of walking on eggshells—literally. "Someone's *got* to start sweeping up after the Swedish Chef, y'all," he fumed.

Well, that would all be another manager's headache now. He was rightly relieved that his days of coddling were nearly over—but there *was* one little lady he would miss: Janice Sorelli, the day's reigning diva of dance and one of the Opera's biggest draws. Her performances as prima ballerina left the normally verbose Grosse blissfully speechless. Ditto for Johnny Fiama, the Opera's leading baritone, with whom she frequently shared the stage but whose romantic intentions she barely noticed.

The free-spirited Janice paid no mind to the public's praise, or to the adolescent crushes of her costars. She was focused on higher planes of existence.

Besides, she already had her eye on a debonair society guy: a handsome frog named Constantine Philippe Georges Marie Comte de Chagny, who had the, like,

---

[1] Construction of the vast complex had taken fourteen years and was completed in 1875. Its opening celebration boasted a spectacular rooftop fireworks display created by the pyrotechnic expert Crazy Harry—despite the fact that nearly fifty crates of shells, rockets, and roman candles had mysteriously gone missing . . .

cutest Russian accent and an adorable mole on his right upper lip. Ironically, Janice's infatuation with the amphibian made Johnny Fiama green with envy.

Tonight, as the gala progressed onstage, Janice was in her serene and spartan dressing room purifying the air with a white-sage smudge stick. The floor was covered in overlapping Indian rugs, and several beanbags were strewn about for seating. On her dressing table she displayed a collection of multicolored crystals, a Chianti bottle with a candle in its neck, and a "Save the Whales" petition she'd been circulating.

Clad in a denim miniskirt, flower-print poncho, and macramé choker, her blond hair pulled into a jaunty side pony, Janice waved a feather to spread the smoke from the smoldering herbs into all the corners. She'd performed a groovy improvised farewell dance as the gala's curtain-raiser and was ready to mellow out. When she was done smudging, she gently tamped the bundle into an oyster shell on her dressing table, snuffing it, and took a seat in lotus pose on her yoga mat. Content in her solitude, she breathed deeply and began to chant "om" on her way into meditation.

Suddenly into her dressing room flocked half a dozen svelte young chickens that had come up from the stage after dancing *La Pulcina Piccola*. They flapped in amid great confusion and a flurry of feathers, some breaking into forced nervous laughter, others letting out sharp squawks and *bawwwwwwwk*s of fear.

Behind them was brash Johnny Fiama, in his doublet and tights, who'd followed their act with an aria, as well as Pepino Rodrigo Serrano Gonzales, a suave king prawn from Milan. Tireless Pepé had first made his name as a stage manager in the opera houses of Spain, where his multiple limbs had proven essential in such a multitasking role.

Startled out of her becalmed state, Janice exclaimed, "*Ooooommmmmmmm*-my gosh!" She staggered to her feet and took in the excited mass. "Like, wow."

The young chicks of the *corps* marveled at the space, for they were accustomed to being lodged in cramped crates where they spent their time clucking and quarreling, snacking on gnats and the occasional gravel pebble until their nightly half-hour calls.

As for Johnny, he was happy in any room with a mirror. Currently, he was staring out from beneath his thick, expressive brows into the looking glass over Janice's dressing table, smoothing his black hair back from his prominent widow's peak, and trying to entice the bohemian babe to glance his way.

But Janice was deliberately ignoring him. She was

very superstitious, as were many theater folk, and one of her beliefs was that if you looked into a mirror for too long, it could steal your soul. She didn't want to risk witnessing something that grody.

It was Camilla—the little chick with the forget-me-not eyes and fetching rose-red wattle—who in a trembling voice finally gave Janice the explanation for the kerfuffle. "Bock bock BEGOWWWK," Camilla squawked. Then, with a *fouetté rond de jambe en tournant*, the dancer swiftly leaped for the dressing-room door. When she landed, she extended a graceful wing and locked the door.

"*Muy* bouncy, Camilla," said Pepé in his charming Spanish accent. "What month were joo hatched?"

Camilla told him April.

"*Sí*, of course—a spring chicken."

"Bock bock BEGOWWWK," Camilla squawked again.[2]

Janice swept aside her long blond bangs, peered at the petrified chick, and said, "Like, what do you mean you actually saw a ghost?"

Janice wished she could laugh off Camilla's creeped-out peep, but she shuddered when she heard it. "So, like,

_____

[2] To the unaccustomed ear, the birds' speech was nothing but an unintelligible series of bawks and clucks. But after so many years of performing with the *corps de poulet*, most of the performers and crew at the Opera generally understood their fowl language.

rilly?" she queried. "You've, like, actually *eyeballed* this phantom you're all going on about?"

Breathless little Camilla nodded. Her twig-like legs were at that moment giving way beneath her, and she dropped with a moan onto a beanbag and promptly laid an egg. Pepé scooped it up with one of his four hands, since J.P. Grosse had been on everyone's cases about the shells (plus the prawn could use it to whip up a nice flan later).

Once Johnny was satisfied that he'd found his best angle in the mirror, he said, "Personally, I feel kinda sorry for that ghost. He's so homely, he should be listed in the *Guinness Book of Ewwwww*."

Janice turned to Johnny. "So you saw him, too?"

"Correctamundo," he said, bestowing upon her his most devastating grin. Hoping to impress her with the bravery of his close encounter, he added, "It was like he walked straight through the wall. It's witchcraft, I tell ya, crazy witchcraft. And I've got no defense for it, the heat is too intense for it . . ."

Janice had tuned him out, though. She was thinking of how the story of the Phantom had inexorably taken hold of the entire Opera family. Everyone was obsessed with the masked figure in a brocade jacket who stalked about the building, from top to bottom, like a shadow;

6

who spoke to nobody, to whom nobody dared speak; and who vanished as soon as he was seen, no one knowing how or to where. Most of the chicks had run across the supernatural being at some point, or so they claimed. After all, it was hard to say who had actually seen him and who hadn't—there were so many overdressed oddballs at the Opera who were *not* ghosts . . .

The truth is that the idea of the Phantom first came from the description given by Beauregard, a dim but diligent janitor at the theater who really and truly *had* seen the ghost. He had encountered it on the little staircase by the footlights, the one that led down to the underground floors known as "the cellars," which were five in number.

To anyone who cared to listen, Beauregard explained in his slow and plodding way: "I'll tell you—it is terrible to behold, you know? Because the thing's skin is blue. Blue!" Hitching up his already high-waisted khakis even higher, he'd go on to describe the creature as something vaguely reptilian, with a pair of horns, each a foot long, that curved off the back of its head, and a thick, kangaroo-like tail that reached all the way down to the floor. Beauregard marveled time and again at the smoke he recalled curling out of its pronounced snout. "And the teeth—sharp as little knifepoints. That's all I could see because a hockey mask covered the rest of its face!"

As he drew his tale to a close, he'd always take off his cap and, befuddled, scratch his furry head. "But the *eyes*—even with that mask I could see the green eyes, like little glowing peas floating in pitch-black oil."

Two things were certain about Beauregard: He always wore a plaid shirt, and he never joked around. So his words were received with interest and amazement. And soon there were others who said that they, too, had been accosted by a vaguely reptilian, green-eyed, blue-skinned creature in a brocade jacket. But the mask it wore to cover so terrifying a face was always different: the Lone Ranger, a sinister clown, an inscrutable King Tut, and so on.

Sensible folks thought that Beauregard may have been the victim of a prank played by a beanpole stagehand named Beaker. But when they asked the guileless ginger if it was true, he frantically proclaimed, "Meep meep meep!" in passionate denial.[3]

And then one after the other came a series of happenings so curious and so inexplicable that even the most skeptical Opera employees were reconsidering.

For instance, few are braver than a firefighter,

---

[3] And as we all now know, Beaker would himself become a victim of perhaps the most famous and well-remembered incident in this whole saga . . .

agreed? They fear nothing, especially not fire (*obvi!*). Well, the fireman in question was an intrepid, floppy-eared elephant named Seymour who could put out even the most raging conflagration with just one trunkful of water. The pachyderm had gone to make a round of code inspections in the cellars, a routine occurrence to ensure that the building's safety was up to snuff.

It seems Seymour had descended to levels he normally didn't. A short while later, he reappeared on the stage, pale and trembling, and practically collapsed into the outstretched arms of Johnny Fiama's mother, Mama Fiama, a deeply dedicated usher at the theater.[4]

And why was Seymour so shaken? Because he had seen coming toward him, floating in the air, a head of fire without a body attached to it!

"Maybe it was Grosse," Pepé suggested at the time. "He ees known for being a hothead, okay. *Hot* head . . . ? Anyone . . . ? No?" Try as he might, Pepé couldn't lighten the ominous mood that permeated the Opera.

The *corps de poulet* was thrown into consternation. This flaming head in no way matched Beauregard's

---

[4] This is recounted in Mama Fiama's memoir, *Ticket Please: The Ups and Downs of Seating People*. It's an exhaustive account of the years she spent at the Opera House as head usher and the keeper of the infamous Box Five. It also includes some of her most rib-sticking recipes, the relevance of which shall come to light shortly.

description of the masked blue-skinned lizard freak. But the young chicks soon accepted the preposterous explanation that the ghost must have several heads that he could swap as he pleased.

And let's face it, once a firefighter fainted, all the creatures of the Opera House had plenty of excuses for the creeping fright that made them quicken their pace when walking down a dark corridor or rounding some blind corner.

You could find the fear even in the Opera's tough-cookie star singer, the powerhouse Yolanda Rat, a no-nonsense rodent who made up for her lack of height with oversize talent and a huge attitude. On the day after she helped revive Seymour alone in her dressing room for about three unforgettable hours (others may have found him chunky, but she found him hunky), she placed a horseshoe on the table by the stage door for everyone to touch before setting foot on the first tread of the staircase, a customary jinx fixer.[5]

But to return to the evening in question: Camilla had seen the ghost, and she was jittery in the extreme. An agonizing silence now reigned in Janice's dressing room. Nothing was heard but the hard breathing of the

---

[5] The shoe didn't remain on the table long, however—the annoyed filly she took it from snatched it back. No one could blame her: It was a Louboutin.

chickens and a robust burp from Pepé, who muttered in apology, "Escuse me. The Swedish Chef's Stroganoff, she ees a real repeater, okay."

Johnny was about to offer Janice a shoulder rub when Camilla, flinging herself into the farthest corner of the room, eyes wide and beak chattering, whispered: *"Bgark!"* And everybody did indeed immediately shush just as the chick had implored. All eyes followed her terrified stare toward the closed dressing-room door.

In the stillness they could hear a faint rustling outside. It was like heavy silk sliding over the door, perhaps the sleeve of an embroidered jacket making gentle contact with the wall's smooth wood . . . Then it stopped.

Janice was determined to show more pluck than the birds. Fighting her fear, she went to the door and tried to sense an aura on the other side of the wood. But getting no vibes, she boldly reached out and turned the key.

Johnny quickly stepped to her side. "Whoa, you don't wanna go out there."

"Aplauso!" cheered Pepé, clapping with all his hands. "Brave Johnny does the chivalry!"

"You got the wrong idea, sea bug. The *bird's* gonna go first." Camilla squawked as Johnny drew back the door and, overlooking her protests, nudged her out into the gloomy hallway, his pinkie rings glinting with reflected light from the bright dressing room behind them.

Beyond Camilla's quivering comb, the baritone saw that the passage seemed to be unoccupied. A gas lamp cast a suspicious light into the surrounding darkness but didn't succeed in dispelling it. All that could be heard were the incongruously upbeat strains of the singing duo Wayne and Wanda warbling a song far away onstage at the ongoing gala performance.

"Fair warning, weirdo," called Johnny to the unseen specter. "Don't make me throw this chicken at you!"

But after a few moments of waiting, Johnny gave up and returned his petrified hostage back inside, closing the door behind them. "There ain't no one there," he announced to the room. "So here's the deal: I'm gonna escort you down to the foyer, and then I by myself solo can bring Janice up here again after. You know, to protect her so she don't have to be alone—capeesh?"

Camilla wasn't convinced. Still quaking, she whispered an appeal to Pepé, who shared her concerns with the group. "She say she ees too afraid she might see him again, the blue demon Beauregard described, okay."

"*Beauregard?* Come on, Peps. That dude's three layers short of a lasagna," scoffed Johnny. "I mean, he *clearly* forgot to pay his brain bill."

Janice bristled. "Like, what makes you say that?"

"One time I come across him frantically painting a scenery flat. I go, 'Why are you moving so fast?' And that brainiac says, 'I wanna get the job done before I run out of paint.'"

"No, ees a fact Beauregard is not the brightest bulb on the shed, okay," agreed Pepé, "but my assistant stage manager, Scooter? He say the story ees true." He told them how the day before, Scooter, alone in the office they shared, had looked up to see the Great Gonzo standing in the doorway.

"Gonzo?" asked Janice, puzzled.

"Joo know him, okay," replied Pepé. "Ees a big opera patron—blue-like-Gatorade fur, eyes that do the bugging out, nose like a dipper gourd?" Janice nodded in recognition, and Camilla brightened—she had been positively pining for this intriguing gent since she first laid eyes on him.

"So anyways," continued Pepé, "Gonzo, he creep out pretty much everyone cuz they think he has the evil eye, which in his case ees both of them. And Scooter, he ees as superstitious as he ees orange." Pepé described how a look of fear appeared on Gonzo's face as he swiftly backed away from Scooter, in the process hitting his head on a hat peg, stumbling backward out of the office, and tumbling down the staircase. "Just a blue ball of fur rolling down the whole first flight," the prawn said, shaking his head. "I'm passing by and I help Gonzo up, because I am the nice guy, okay." Expecting the worst, Pepé was actually surprised by Gonzo's reaction. "He shout, 'That was *awesome*! I wanna do it again!' *Porque* he *live* for the dangerous daredevil stuff." And here he lowered his voice, recounting how at that point he asked Gonzo to tell him what had just frightened him so, but the blue dude refused. Then they looked up to see Scooter at the top of the stairs and—here he couldn't suppress a shudder—right behind Scooter stood *the ghost*. "The lizardy ghost with the glowing green *ojos*, okay!"

A series of churlish chirps from Camilla prompted Janice to respond, "But, like, why do you say Scooter and Gonzo and Beauregard should hold their tongues?"

"Aww, that's not *her* opinion," replied Pepé. "Ees her father's. He think the ghost might want to, how joo say? 'Swim under the radar,' okay. He think the *fantasma* does not want the attention."

The bird explained haltingly that she had promised her father—who was at the gala on this very night and who might be popping backstage any minute—that she would keep her beak shut on the matter. But this reticence further stoked the curiosity of the young chicks, who crowded around Camilla, begging her to explain herself till finally, burning to say all she knew, her eyes fixed on the door, she spilled it with two clucks.

"The box?" repeated Janice. "What box?"

Camilla told her she meant a private box at the Opera. Balcony Box Five on the Grand Tier, to be specific.

"Oh yeah," said Johnny, "that's the one my ma's in charge of."

Camilla told them that her father had a season subscription for Box Six, right next to Box Five. But here she broke off and insisted that they all pinkie-claw swear that what she was going to reveal would not go beyond this room.

When they had done so, Camilla whispered the remainder of her tale to Pepé, for fear she'd be overheard in the hallway by her father, and the prawn relayed it to the rest. "She say that Box Five ees the ghost's box, and for as long as anyone can remember, nobody but the ghost has had it. The box office was told not to sell the seats to anyone else."

Thereupon little Camilla began to sob, blubbering that she should have said nothing, that if her father found out, he'd have her filleted and fried. She insisted that Beauregard, Scooter, and Gonzo should never have talked of things that didn't concern them and that surely it would bring bad juju to them all.

Just then there was the sound of hurried and heavy footsteps approaching in the passage and an out-of-breath "Bgark buk buk *bgark*!"

Camilla nearly crumbled as her imposing dad opened the door. The normally refined rooster bustled into the dressing room and dropped, groaning, onto a vacant beanbag. The others all cried out in concern, and Camilla went and roosted next to him. Her flustered father clucked mournfully, saying something dreadful about a janitor.

"Do you mean Beauregard?" ventured Janice.

"He ees *muerto*?" asked Pepé, incredulous.

The room was filled with astonished outcries and scared requests for explanations of Beauregard's demise. The rooster continued, fanning himself lightly with one wing tip and explaining that the body was found in the third-floor cellar, apparently quite sandwiched between two scenery flats.

"*Heavy*," Janice said with a sigh.

Johnny wondered if now was the right time to offer her the shoulder massage.

But before he could propose it, general pandemonium struck outside in the hallway. For the horrid news had quickly spread throughout the backstage area. The dressing rooms emptied, and the *corps*, a frightened

16

flock crowding around Janice, made its way en masse through the ill-lit passages and staircases toward the foyer, scurrying as fast as their little chicken feet could carry them.

Chapter II

THE MAGNIFICENT "MAHNA MAHNA"

On the first landing, Janice and the petrified pack ran into Comte Constantine de Chagny, a respected amphibian aristocrat with the string of names to prove it, bounding up the stairs three at a time. Though he was resolutely French, Constantine had been very close to one of the nannies who helped raise him; she hailed from Saint Petersburg, and her charge had somehow picked up her Russian accent and passion for pierogi. Typically quite stoic and collected, the intriguing society frog was now grinning and greatly excited.

"Vas just cominx to praise your dance," Constantine said to Janice, politely taking off his top hat. "And my brother, Monsieur Viscount Kermit de Chagny, was deeply moved by song of Piggy Daaé."

"Piggy Daaé? No way!" said Johnny, who was shamelessly competitive with his fellow performers at the Opera. "Six weeks ago she had a voice that sounded like silverware in a garbage disposal. I mean, her singing is so shaky, she'd have to perform in Key West to know for sure what key she was in."

Janice placed a hand on the frog's forearm. "Listen, I'm rilly sorry, Connie, but we're on our way to find out how our janitor Beauregard bit it."

Sam Eagle, the Opera House's by-the-book business manager, who boasted fine feathers everywhere except his head, was hurrying by when he heard this remark. He stopped and exclaimed, "I beg your pardon! How did you hear the secret?"

"'Secret'? Oh please," said Pepé. "It ees all over the Facebooks already, okay."

"Well, do forget about it for tonight—and above all don't mention it to J.P. It would upset him too much on his last day and ruin the party. And that would be positively unpatriotic."

"Upset J.P.? I do not think that ees gonna happen," said Pepé. "Paying one less salary will make that pincher of pennies *muy*, *muy* happy. Am I right or am I right, Baldy?"

Sam continued on his way, waving a wing dismissively and calling back, "Just keep it to yourself, you rapscallion. Have some dignity."

"Oh, I have the dignity," called Pepé, piqued. "And

while eagles may soar, Señor Sam, we prawns do not get sucked into jet engines! So there!" But the big bird had already turned the corner.

They all proceeded into the foyer, which was full of patrons milling around, buzzing about the impressive program they'd just seen. Comte Constantine de Chagny was right: It was clear that no Opera House performance had ever equaled this one. Still, the evening's unanimous triumph was Mademoiselle Piggy Daaé, who had astonished the audience. Clad in a red satin strapless gown, her lustrous honey-blond locks in bouncy barrel curls, the Scandinavian songstress had wowed the crowd with the superhuman notes she hit on "Mahna Mahna," which she sang in the place of Yolanda, who on this evening was inexplicably ill.

No one had ever heard anything like it. Piggy revealed a new splendor, a radiance hitherto unsuspected. The whole house went mad, cheering, clapping, holding their lighters above their heads. Over the din Kermit de Chagny, the handsome younger brother of Constantine, had blissfully yelled, "Yayyyyyyyyyyy!" He and Piggy had known each other long ago as children, and he'd watched from afar as her star had begun to rise at the Opera.

Onstage, Piggy basked in the crowd's adulation. Finally, when they hushed to hear her speak, she took a pause in the charged silence and finally declared, "You like *moi*! You *really* like *moi*!" Then she fully fainted into the arms of her fellow singers and had to be hoisted to her dressing room by the crew of penguin stagehands.

It was a perfect star-is-born storm. And it had required Yolanda Rat's incomprehensible and inexcusable absence from this gala night for the up-and-comer, at a moment's warning, to deliver the goods.

Constantine had stood in his box with his younger brother, joining all this frenzy by loudly applauding. The siblings were the source of much society interest, which dated back to the sad passings of their father and mother. Constantine was now the head of one of the oldest and most distinguished frog families in the marshy Le Marais area, on the banks of the Seine.

Finding themselves suddenly parentless, Constantine had become a father figure to his sibling. Although Kermit was now a little over twenty-one, he still looked younger, thanks to a robust skin-care routine and daily application of SPF. He was above average height and in excellent physical health, owing in no small part to a strict diet of organic bugs and cold-pressed swamp juices. He had kind eyes sitting atop his well-shaped head along with a fetching chartreuse complexion, and, if you squinted, you could maybe make out a peach-fuzz mustache.

Both the Chagny brothers, already amphibious by nature, exhibited a taste for the sea. At Constantine's urging, Kermit had entered the French Naval Academy, finished his courses with honors, and was now preparing to take his required voyage to the North Pole. Each year the graduates sailed and each year the graduates failed in their mission to find Kris Kringle's home and base of Yuletide operations. So they kept trying, year after year.

Until then, Kermit was enjoying a long six-month furlough. Constantine took advantage of Kermit's leave of absence by doing some manly-man bonding with him at all the most macho spots in Paris: the boxing matches, the billiard halls, the racetrack, and, of course, the opera. Which is where we pick up with them again, applauding Piggy's perfect performance of "Mahna Mahna."

Constantine turned to Kermit and saw that his green face had paled from chartreuse to sage. "Don't you see," said Kermit, "that she has fainted?"

"Vat is goink on here? Is lookink to me like you yourself are almost faintink," joked the count.

"Let's go backstage and make sure she's okay," Kermit pleaded. "She never sang like that before."

It now dawned on Constantine why Kermit was sometimes absentminded when spoken to and why he always tried to turn every conversation back to the subject of the opera: His little bro was gaga over the gal!

The siblings soon passed through the door leading from the audience to the stage, making their way through the crowd of stagehands waddling about and performers awaiting their cues.[6] Kermit led the way, feeling that his heart no longer belonged to him, his face set with passion, while Constantine followed with a big smile. They had to pause before the cacophonous, clucking inrush of the *corps de poulet*, who blocked the passage they were trying to enter.

The count was surprised to find that Kermit knew where he was going. He had never before taken him to Piggy's dressing room, and he came to the conclusion that the little sneak must have gone there alone on past evenings while Constantine himself had lingered to flirt with that hot hippie Janice Sorelli.

Postponing his usual tête-à-tête with Janice for a few minutes tonight, the count followed his brother down the passage that led to Piggy's dressing room and saw that it was crammed—the whole audience, it seemed, was as excited by her success as by her fainting fit.

Everyone parted as Bunsen Honeydew, the house

---

[6] Subscribers to the Opera were given the privilege of going to certain backstage areas before, during, and after performances, where they could soak up the showbiz ambiance and snap selfies with the stars.

doctor for the theater, arrived. Kermit trailed into the room in the doc's wake, and as luck would have it, he caught the zaftig singer in his arms as she swooned yet again. Honeydew seemed surprised that the frog's sticklike legs didn't buckle—that pig was not petite.

"Don't you think, Doctor, that these admirers should probably clear the room?" asked Kermit pointedly as he rested Piggy on a settee. "There's no air in here."

"You're quite right," said Dr. Honeydew, his eyes behind his black-framed spectacles inscrutably small as he concentrated on what he was hearing through his stethoscope. "Her heart is about to beat right out of her chest."

"Um," said Kermit, "that's *my* heart."

"Yes! Quite right again," said Honeydew, switching the chestpiece from Kermit to Piggy. After a moment, he said, "Well, her pulse is also elevated."

"It's elevated?! What could that possibly *mean*?"

"Up," explained Honeydew. Then he sent everyone away. Constantine departed with a wave and a wink to Kermit, who remained in the room, cradling the singer as she slowly returned to life.

The frog watched as the doctor set up an easel, placed a canvas on it, and took out some colored pencils. "What are you doing now?"

"I'm preparing to draw blood."

Just then Piggy uttered a deep sigh, which was answered by a little ribbit. She turned her head, saw Kermit, and started. She looked at Dr. Honeydew, then at Kermit again. "*Pardonnez-moi*," she said, in a voice not much above a whisper, "but who are *vous*?"

"Hi ho, mademoiselle," replied Kermit, bending one frog leg to kneel on one frog knee and press one fervent, frog-lipped kiss on the back of the budding diva's hand. He was searching for the right words, but not finding them. He finally uttered, "I can't feel my face when I'm with you . . . and I love it."

Piggy began to giggle.

Though he was embarrassed, Kermit wasn't about to give up. "Piggy," he said firmly, "I am the little froglet who went into the sea to rescue your Jet Ski!" She didn't respond, so he persisted, changing his tack: "I'd like to say something to you in private, something very important."

She shook her head. "How about a rain check?"

"Yes, you better go," said the doctor, sternly but with his pleasantest smile. "Leave me to attend to mademoiselle."

"No," Piggy suddenly protested, standing up. "I'm fine, I'm really fine. Watch this." With a half-hearted "*hiiiiii-YA*," she executed a wobbly karate chop to the air. "See? I'm feeling so much stronger now. All I need is some carbs and I'll be back to normal. You boys go ahead and hit the road. Go on." She poured it on: "Pretty please *avec une cerise sur le dessus?*"

The doctor made a short protest, but, perceiving the pig's evident agitation, he thought the best remedy was not to thwart her. He departed, ushering out Kermit as well and saying to him with concern when they were outside in the hallway, "It's very disconcerting. She is absolutely not herself tonight."

"Because she's pained?"

"No, because she's polite." Then he said *bonne nuit* and excused himself. Kermit was left alone.

The whole of this area of the theater was now deserted. Though Kermit knew the farewell ceremony was continuing onstage, he found it curiously quiet. He thought Piggy might return to watch the remainder of the performances, so he waited in the silent solitude, hiding in the shadow of a doorway. He closed his eyes and felt a terrible pain in his heart. It was about this in particular that he wanted to speak to her.

"So joo wait for the autograph, *sí?*"

Kermit looked up to find a king prawn standing in front of him, holding costumes. "I beg your pardon?"

"Joo wait here for Señora Piggy to sign her John

Hancock on joor *Playbill*, no? That ees why joo do the lurking around like the stalker?"

"No, no, you've got it wrong, my dear crustacean. I am no stalker. Piggy and I, well . . . we are in love," confessed Kermit.

"Oh, well, if it ees the love, *que romántico*. I love the love. And she loves joo, too?"

"She . . . does. At least I think she does," Kermit said, his brain beginning to work again. "She asked to be alone. She wanted everyone to leave, even the doctor. Because—because . . . because she wanted to be left alone *for me*! Didn't I tell her that I wanted to speak to her privately? And hey—she cleared the room!"

"Well, knock joorself out, amigo, and leave this with her, *por favor*," said the stranger, handing him a costume he had hemmed, then hustling down the hallway humming a hymn.

Hardly breathing, Kermit tiptoed to the dressing room and, with his ear to the door to catch Piggy's reply, prepared to knock. But he dropped his hand. Because he heard—could it be?—*a male voice* inside, saying, in a posh English accent, "Are you sleepy, my pet?"

Kermit heard Piggy sigh and reply, *"Seriously?!"* She paused to crunch on something, surely her snack, then continued. "Tonight I gave you and that audience my

28

whole soul, and I am freakin' wiped out!"

"And I thank you, my dear. That is a gift that I treasure. And the Koozebanians surely treasure it, too."

Koozebanians? Where have I heard that word before . . . wondered Kermit.

He returned to his dark corner, determined to wait for this interloper to leave the room.

Piggy soon emerged alone, dressed in a tailored trench coat, black beret, and modest five-inch stilettos. She closed the door behind her, but keen-eyed Kermit observed that she didn't lock it.

She passed his hiding spot and he didn't dare follow her, even with his eyes, for his focus was fixed on the door, which did not open again.

When Piggy was long gone and only the fragrance of Corn Nuts lingered in the passage, he slipped into the dressing room and shut the door. He was in absolute darkness—until the glowing screen of a smartphone lit up the room.

Kermit jumped and saw that it was Pepé holding the device. The frog whispered, "Where did *you* come from?"

"Spain."

"No, I meant just now. You move really quick."

"I have the many limbs," said Pepé, ostentatiously displaying them. "Are joo looking for something? Because

I do not think joo are supposed to be in here."

"Neither is *he*!"

"Who?"

"There's someone in here!"

"Yeah: joo. And now me, too." Pepé took the costume from Kermit and draped it over the chair.

"And someone else! I heard him." Kermit addressed the room in a quavering voice. "All right, come out and put up your dukes, you hear!"

They stood for several long moments listening to the silence of the empty room.

"Maybe he feel embarrassed, okay, because he leave his dukes at home?"

"Good grief," Kermit said, "am I going out of my mind?"

"I think where joo are going ees *home*, okay," ventured the prawn as he ushered Kermit out of the room and locked the door behind them before disappearing down the hallway.

Kermit was stumped. Where could his unseen rival have disappeared to? Did he *imagine* the whole thing?

Finally, he started walking, not knowing what he was doing nor where he was going. At one point in his aimless wandering of the mazelike hallways, an icy draft struck his face. He found himself on a staircase, up which a procession of paramedic sheep were carrying a mound covered with a white sheet on a makeshift stretcher.

"Which is the way out, please?" he asked one of them.

The shaggy ram answered, "*Baaaaaaaa*-ck behind you, boss. The door's open. But let us go by first."

Pointing at the stretcher, Kermit asked, "What's that?"

Another sheep replied, "*That* is Beauregard, who was found in the third cellar, deceased."

"How horrible!" exclaimed Kermit. "What was the cause?"

"Squishing."

Added the ram, "It seems he was smushed right between two flats painted with scenes from *Death in Venice*."

Kermit took off his hat and brought his hands to his face, shaking his head. "Goodness gracious," he said, looking somber. "That is just . . . so terribly . . . meta."

Then he fell back to make room for the procession, which continued on its grim way.

Chapter III

SOMETHING WORSE THAN THIEVES

During this time, the farewell ceremony for the retiring manager, J.P. Grosse, had continued, as the majority of the attendees were as yet unaware of the brewing drama with the now-belated Beauregard.

It was a monumental event. Grosse was the central core for all the cultural networking in Paris, the Opera being the city's primary social hub, so his farewell was the must-attend shindig of the season. Everyone who was anyone was there. So were no ones who wanted to be someones.

All these glitterati and wannabes met for the after-party in the main foyer, where the DJ was warming up the crowd with "Who Let the Dogs Out." His pièce de résistance involved releasing an actual pack of dogs on the dancers. That always got them moving.

In the next room, the members of the *corps de poulet* were discussing the bizarre developments of the day while keeping their beady eyes on the supper tables arranged about the space, eagerly awaiting the Swedish Chef's promised meatballs and lingonberry sauce. The chicks were feeling peckish.[7]

A handful of dancers had already changed out of their costumes and fluffed up their feathers, but many still wore their tulle skirts. All of them, however, had remembered to put on a respectfully somber expression for the occasion.

But not ambitious Johnny Fiama, who couldn't resist working the crowd, having apparently forgotten both the tragic squishing of Beauregard and the option of changing out of his tights. Johnny was a firm believer in self-promotion, something his single-minded mother had instilled in him, and he took every opportunity to try to further his career. When Grosse walked into view on the steps of the foyer—wearing his best pin-striped suit with his signature carnation in the buttonhole, and trailed by his nephew, Scooter, and his faithful secretary, a scrappy rat named Rizzo—Johnny finally put the glad-handing on hold.

This evening, Grosse was in a jolly mood, delighted to

---

[7] I unearthed the Swedish Chef's handwritten notes for the evening's menu, which also included pickled herring smørrebrød, toast skagen, and oven-baked cod in ümlaut sauce.

finally be leaving his taxing job, but Scooter, in his black round-framed glasses and the favorite green satin jacket he always wore, was feeling decidedly maudlin about his uncle's departure. Grosse had indulged the kid earlier when he got weepy and said he needed to hug it out.

Suddenly Camilla bellowed a big *bawk* in a tone of unspeakable terror that shattered the festive mood.

With a trembling wing, she pointed among the crowd of dandies to a freaky figure wearing a brocade jacket and a shiny black Darth Vader helmet over his head. The gag was immediately deemed a hit. "It's the Phantom!" everyone gaily cried. Added a reveler, "'I am a ghost, and *I am your father*!'" They mocked the rumors of a specter in their midst. (No one seemed to notice the powder-blue hue of its neck and hands or the thick tail protruding from its backside . . .) They laughed and nudged their neighbors and wanted to offer this comically costumed character a drink—but just like that, he was gone.

The others hunted in vain for him while Grosse, who was wildly allergic to dander, put on a not-very-convincing show of trying, from as far away as possible, to calm Camilla. She did not seem to be in on the joke, for she stood shrieking like a pummeled peacock. Grosse tasked Scooter with quieting the chick and disappeared into the crowd as fast as the ghost himself.

Eventually the Swedish Chef rang the dinner bell and announced, "Tøøm to makin vit de gøøble eetin!" Everyone—including Grosse's successors, the imposingly crotchety Messieurs Statler and Waldorf—took their seats at the tables.

At the retiring manager's behest, Rizzo gave Statler and Waldorf the two tiny master keys that opened all the Opera House's 2,531 doors over the whole of its seventeen levels. [8]

"That's a lot of doors," marveled Waldorf, who turned to Statler and said, "Knock knock!"

"Who's there?" Statler answered.

"A little girl."

"A little girl who?"

"A little girl who can't reach the doorbell!"

The duo chortled, but their laughter trailed off when they spied, at the end of their table, a creature in the same brocade jacket as the Darth Vader who had been glimpsed earlier—sitting there as natural as could be, except that he neither ate nor drank. Those who began by looking at him with a convivial smile ended by turning their heads. No one repeated the joviality of the foyer this time.

---

[8] Though there were some doors that only one individual at the Opera House knew about, and entry to those required something quite a bit more creative than a commonplace key . . .

For this time there was *no mask*.

Among the members of this rather superficial crowd, most felt that his visage was terrifying, like a mash-up of crocodile and Komodo dragon that had been dusted with a pale blue powder. A pair of horns, shaped like the Grim Reaper's scythe blade, curved off the back of his head. Wisps of smoke trailed out of his sizable nostrils, and his pea-size eyes glowed an unnatural green in haunting black sockets, like twin alien planets in deepest space.

"Must be a Grosse friend," whispered Statler to Waldorf.

"I'd say it's his grossest," his partner replied.

The blue lizard-dragon himself did not speak a word, and his closest neighbors could not have stated at what precise moment he had sat down between them. The friends of J.P. Grosse likely thought that this oddity was an acquaintance of Statler and Waldorf, while Statler and Waldorf's friends must have believed that the peculiarly prehistoric creature belonged to Grosse's party.[9]

The upshot is that no one asked for an explanation; no one made an unpleasant remark; no joke in bad taste was made that might have offended. A few of those who

_____

[9] Oh, who are we kidding—Statler and Waldorf had no friends.

knew the description Beauregard had given of the ghost thought that the thing at the end of the table might easily have passed for it.

Grosse, sitting at the center of the table, did not see the ghoul until suddenly it spoke to him, in a slow, overripe English accent: "I might as well confirm that the ballet chicks are spot-on, Mr. Manager. The flattening of that meddlesome Beauregard is perhaps not an accident."

Grosse gave a start. "What in tarnation do you mean, 'flattening'? Is Beauregard hurt?"

"Worse," purred the creature. "He's gone into the fertilizer business."

"He's gone into— What do you mean?"

"He's bought the farm."

"What farm?"

"He's checked in to the horizontal Hilton."

Grosse was baffled. "He went on vacation?"

"Blimey! All my evil wit is lost on you! Those are *euphemisms*—Beauregard is dead!"

Grosse turned pale. He rose from his chair and stared strangely at the speaker. At last, he made an urgent gesture to Statler and Waldorf. They each muttered a few words of excuse to the guests as they followed him into the manager's office with Rizzo trailing.

I leave it to Statler to complete the story. In his *Memoirs*,[10] he wrote:

> *Once we got behind closed doors, Grosse rubbed his temples and asked Waldorf and I if we knew who we had all just seen. When we said no, he took the master keys from me, stared at them for a moment, and said something. No idea what. So I adjusted my hearing aid and asked him to repeat himself. He advised us to have new locks made for all the doors in the Opera.*
>
> *Waldorf asked with a sly grin, "Why? Has someone stolen more than just the spotlight?"*
>
> *"There is somethin' worse than thieves," Grosse replied in his drawl.*
>
> *"And what is that?" I asked.*
>
> *"A phantom," said Grosse gravely, and behind him Rizzo's nose twitched as he nodded in agreement.*
>
> *This really got us giggling. They had to be pulling our legs. Grosse was miffed. "Cain't you be serious already?"*
>
> *I told him that yes, we technically can, we just prefer not to.*

---

[10] Statler penned his extensive *Memoirs* during the fairly long period of his management. In fact, they were *so* extensive that we may well ask how he ever found time to actually do his job. Still, it was a very fortuitous happenstance in the creating of this account. So a hat tip to you, Statler, old chum!

"I wouldn't never'a brang up the ghost," he continued, *"if I hadn't gotten an order from the kook himself to ask y'all to be nice to him."*

"You've got a phantom that gives you orders?" asked Waldorf.

"Trust me: You'd better do what he says or you'll be sorry."

"Look," I said to Grosse, *"I wasn't born yesterday."*

"You weren't even born this century," quipped Waldorf. *"The upside of that is that I can go to your birthday party and warm myself by the cake!"*

I paid no attention to him. "J.P.," I said, "we know what you're up to." I explained that Waldorf and I had pulled off some pretty impressive gags in our time. In college we basically majored in practical jokes. And we were copresidents of our fraternity, Delta Lotta Pranks. So you're not going to find us easily falling for others' tricks.

I could see that Waldorf was amused by all this, though some of the fun was sapped because of this fellow Beauregard's apparent end—I say "apparent" because at that point we weren't even sure anyone had been flattened. I mean, how were we to know that Grosse wasn't just hazing the newbies? We finally couldn't help bursting out laughing.

Grosse looked at us in disbelief, reiterating, "This is serious."

"So is trigonometry," I replied, *"but that doesn't make it any more interesting."*

He was clearly not giving up, so I said to him, "The question is, just what exactly does this ghost of yours want?"

"And the answer is, who cares?" Waldorf interjected with mirth in his eyes.

"You better care, gents," warned Grosse. "Rizzo, grab the memorandum book."

"Roger that," said the rat, and he retrieved an official-looking government tome from the shelf and hoisted it onto the table before them. He opened it to the page relating that anyone who managed the Opera was bound to "give to all productions the splendor that becomes the most important stage in France." I noticed that it was followed by a paragraph scrawled by hand in red ink.

"Them there are the ghost's demands," said Grosse.

The rat cleared his throat and read: "'The manager, in any month, must not delay for more than two weeks the payment of the allowance to the Phantom of the Opera of twenty thousand francs a month.'"

"So you rent your ghost like a party clown?" asked Waldorf, still trying to keep a straight face. "Is that all? Or does he want more than that? A bouncy castle, maybe?"

"Oh, you can bet he wants more," replied Grosse.

And Rizzo read on. "Box Five on the Grand Tier shall be held for the Phantom for every performance. Honor this. Do not get yourself into a sticky wicket."

When we saw this, there was nothing else for us to do but stand (easier said than done at our age), shake our predecessor by the hand, and congratulate him on thinking up this little joke. Waldorf added that he now understood why Grosse was retiring: Business was impossible with such a greedy ghost as part of the staff! He said: "You should fire him, or have him arrested—"

"How in heaven's name am I supposed to pull that off?" Grosse said, exasperated. "I'd never even laid eyes on the thing before he showed up out there at the table tonight!"

"What about when he comes to his box?"

"Um, hel-LO?! Are you listening to me? I've never seen him in his box 'cause I've never seen him, period. Till now."

"So sell the seats."

"Sell the seats in the Phantom's box! Well, fellas, you feel free to try it. I'm washing my hands of this mess, and good luck to you."

Grosse left the office with Rizzo at his heels. But before the rat crossed the threshold, he turned back and said quite seriously, "I'll do my best to help ya, but this phantom is a real humdinger. I got a few tricks up my sleeve I'd be willin' to share . . . if the price is right."

"The price?"

"See, I'm paid in cheese, so if there was maybe an extra wheel or two of gorgonzola in the picture, I could be persuaded

to enlighten the situation. Mull it over." And out he went.

Well, well, well. Fleeced for cheese by a rat—that was a new one!

Apart from that time we gave those excited trick-or-treaters our homemade caramel onions, Waldorf and I had never laughed so much in our lives.

I have you received a reply from that girl Daaé, to my letter asking for an explanation, and it proves that you did indeed know all about my memorandum book additions and, consequently, that you are treating me with outrageous contempt. If you wish to live in peace, you must not begin by taking away my private box...

Believe me to be,
Dear Mr. Managers,
Deadly Serious

The Phantom

Chapter IV

BOX FIVE GETS BIZARRO

So, you may ask, who were these new Opera House bosses, anyway, and how did they get such plum jobs? Well, Statler may not have known a note of music, but he had been a skilled networker and he boasted a very robust LinkedIn profile. He had landed a hefty inheritance when his parents passed away late in life in a freak tapioca accident. And though his caustic sense of humor rubbed some the wrong way, he was not lacking in savvy. For as soon as he made up his mind to throw his hat into the ring to take over the Opera, he picked the best possible partner with whom to share the endeavor: his old college chum Waldorf.

Waldorf was a very distinguished composer who had published a number of successful pieces of all kinds, from hit songs for boy bands to cunning little earworm jingles for commercials. (You know a certain burger joint's signature "I'm lovin' it"? Credit—or blame—him.)

He shared a curmudgeonly streak similar to Statler's, and when it came to others' work, he was pretty much impossible to please. Not shy about sharing his opinion, Waldorf was widely feared for his often-withering critiques. It was, however, the duty of every ambitious performer to now work at pleasing him.

The first few days that the partners spent at the Opera were filled with gloating over the fact that they were the head of so magnificent an enterprise. They had all but forgotten the fantastic story of the Phantom when an incident occurred that proved to them that the joke was apparently still in play.

Waldorf reached his office that morning at ten o'clock. Rizzo, who had retained his role as secretary, handed Waldorf half a dozen letters that had arrived for the managers. "Ya might wanna start with this one," said the rat ominously. The envelope was addressed in telltale red ink. Waldorf opened it.[11]

Good day, dear Managers:

So sorry to have to trouble you at a time

---

[11] After the ordeal at the Opera House had concluded, Rizzo collected all the managers' correspondence. Unfortunately, his idea of archiving it involved using the papers to pad his nest in the sewer. Thankfully, a few key pieces, including this one, were salvaged.

when you must be very busy, renewing important engagements, signing fresh ones, and generally displaying your excellent taste. I know what has been done for Yolanda Rat, Janice Sorelli, and a few others in whom the management has seen admirable qualities.

Of course, when I say "admirable qualities," I do not mean to apply them to La Yolanda, who sings like a cow who just stepped on her udder; nor to Janice, who plods about like a scarecrow that's lost its stuffing.

Inexplicably, Mademoiselle Piggy has not been on the short list, though her genius (and très chic fashion sense) are unquestionable. Why she earns only minor roles and must endure the thankless task of understudying is beyond me. But perhaps it is Yolanda's jealousy that prevents Piggy from winning any important part. That rodent's stabbed more people in the back than sciatica.

But who am I to carp? After all, you are free to conduct your little business as you think best, are you not?

All the same, I should like to take advantage of the fact that you have not yet turned Piggy out of doors by letting her sing the small but key part of Siebel in Faust *this evening. It's time she was allowed the chance to shine. And I will ask you to reserve my box tonight and all following nights, for I cannot end this letter without telling you how disagreeably surprised I have been to discover that my box has been sold to the unwashed masses, and apparently by your orders.*

I did not protest, first, because as much as I like my masses washed, I like avoiding scandal and undue scrutiny even more; and, second, because I thought that your predecessor, J.P. Grosse, who was always respectful to me, might have neglected, before leaving, to mention my little needs to you.

I have now received a reply from that gentleman to my letter asking for an explanation, and it proves that you did indeed know all about my memorandum-book additions and, consequently, that you are treating me with outrageous contempt. If you wish to live in peace, you must not begin by taking away my private box.

Believe me to be, dear Mr. Managers,
Deadly Serious, The Phantom.

The letter was accompanied by a torn-out corner of a page from the classifieds of the *Revue Théâtrale*. Waldorf looked it over.

Missing: Our pet skunk, Miss Beelzebub, escaped from her fortified basement closet, broke a double-paned window with her teeth, and clawed through a stone wall. She's super cuddly and great with babies. She just has a few little anger issues. (Return to 74 rue Dulong.)

For Sale: Parachute. Only used once, never opened, small stain. (Inquire at 33 boulevard Diderot.)

Dear Mister Phantom: There ain't no excusin' Statler and Waldorf. I told 'em exactly what you asked me to and left your dadgum memorandum book in their hands. Scout's honor.—J.P.G.

Waldorf had hardly finished reading this letter when Statler entered the office, carrying one exactly the same. They looked at each other and smiled. "Well, it looks like he's not letting go of the joke," said Waldorf. "Do you find this amusing?"

"No, but when do I find *anything* in this theater

amusing?" cracked Statler, shrugging off his cape.

"Does Grosse think that just because he's been manager of the Opera, we're going to let him have a box whenever he wants it?"

"I'd like to give him a box—right on the ear!" said Statler with a raised fist and a chortle.

"It's harmless enough, I guess. Let's see if he comes to the performance, or if he keeps up this demented talk of haunting. Rizzo, this afternoon let's deliver a ticket to Box Five on the Grand Tier to Grosse."

"Ten-four, boss," said the rat.

"Where does he live, anyway?" Statler wondered aloud with a suspicious tone.

Rizzo pawed through an address book. "Corner of the rue Scribe and the boulevard des Capucines. And hey—whattaya know: These two letters were mailed from the boulevard des Capucines post office."

"Aha, you see?" said Waldorf. "He's a prankster!"

Rizzo said, "Uh, I dunno about that. It doesn't sound like J.P. *His* idea of fun was formatting an Excel spreadsheet. Nerd alert!"

Waldorf chuckled. "To think that such a tightwad would spring for an ad in the *Revue Théâtrale*!"

"You know," said Statler, rereading the letter, "he seems pretty obsessed with that little Piggy."

"She's got a solid reputation," said Waldorf.

"Reputations are easy to get. Don't I have a reputation for knowing all about music? And I don't know one key from another."

"Don't worry: You never had that reputation," Waldorf declared to Statler and Rizzo's delight.

Thereupon they ordered their secretary to usher in the artists, who for the last two hours had been pacing outside the door behind which fame and fortune—or humiliating rejection—awaited. First up was Big Tiny Tallsaddle, a tenor known for his Texas twang. Statler and Waldorf were not fans of twang.

They spent the rest of their day negotiating contracts, and in some cases canceling them (happy trails, Big Tiny!). The two overworked managers went to bed early, forgetting to even glance at Box Five to see whether Grosse was enjoying the performance.

The next morning, they received a card in the mail:

Hullo, my dear Managers:

What a capital evening! And all thanks to Piggy, who was exquisite as Siebel. Yolanda, per usual, was utterly commonplace. Surely I'm not the only one who prefers a Margarita with some kick?

*I shall write you soon for the 20,000 francs—
or 13,549 francs, to be fair. Monsieur Grosse had
already sent me 6,451, representing the first ten
days of my allowance for the current year, and his
privileges finished on the evening of the tenth.*

*Toodeloo,
The Phantom.
P.S.: I loooove maths!*

"Well, well. He writes *maths* with an *s*," exclaimed
Statler. "I knew our ghost was a twit, but now we also
know he's a Brit!"

The morning post also included a letter from Grosse:

*Fellas,
Much obliged for your kind thought, but I'm
sure you'll understand that the idea of listening to
Faust again, as much as I love a good deal-with-
the-devil yarn, can't make me forget that I'm not
allowed to take Box Five. Better not toy with the
Phantom. He has a very peculiar sense of humor.
Say howdy to Rizzo for me. I miss our Excel
marathons.
J.P.G.*

"Oh, this buffoon is getting on my last nerve!"

"Careful, Statler, you don't want to wind up with shingles again."

That evening, they told the box office to sell tickets for the seats in Box Five. That oughta show him, they thought. But they thought wrong . . .

When Statler and Waldorf arrived in their office the next morning, Rizzo told them that the Opera's security guard, Clueless Morgan, a galumphing goat who unfortunately lived up to his first name, was waiting to speak to them.

Although Clueless was terrible at his job, Grosse had apparently kept him on staff for economic reasons: On his lunch hour, Clueless would double as a groundskeeper, happily eating the weeds outside the Opera House and saving Grosse an extra salary.

"Well, out with it," barked Statler bluntly when Clueless sidestepped into the room, his short-brimmed hat askew.

Clueless blinked a few times and stroked his mottled little chin beard, then realized they were talking to him. "Oh! Well, it's about a thing that happened in Box Five last night. See, mister, these darn hooligans that had bought seats in the box, the moment after they gone in, they come out again and hollered for the box keeper, Mama Fiama. They says, 'Look in the box: There's no one there, is there? Well, when we went in, we heard a voice saying, *This box is taken!*' " Clueless blinked and stared at the gents.

Statler could not help but smile as he looked at Waldorf, but Waldorf didn't smile back. As a veteran mischief maker, he recognized in the guard's story all the marks of one of those practical gags that begin by amusing the victims and end by enraging them.

Clueless, to curry favor with Statler, thought it best to return his smile—which turned out to be a very bad idea: Three discolored teeth protruded grotesquely over his lower lip, his face scrunched into a grimace, and as he exhaled, he gave Waldorf a big sour blast of alfalfa breath. The elderly gentleman glared at the goat, who thenceforth made every effort to keep his lips pressed together, giving the unfortunate impression that he was either vaguely chagrined or terribly constipated.

"So when these 'hooligans' arrived," clarified Waldorf, "there was no one in the box, was there?"

"Nope! Not a soul in the box on the right or in the box on the left, cross my heart!"

"And what did the usher say?"

"Oh, Mama Fiama said that it was reserved for the Phantom," said Clueless, accidentally grinning again.

Waldorf went from gloomy to furious, and shouted, "Get her this minute!"

Rizzo stood. "All right already, I'm on it. Don't get your undies in a bundle."

After the secretary exited, Waldorf pressed Clueless: "Have *you* ever seen this 'Phantom'?"

But the bashful billy was by this time incapable of speaking a word. He gave a vigorous shake of the head, sending a string of drool sailing into the air.

The Opera's somber business manager, Sam Eagle, entered the room, and Waldorf paid no more attention to Clueless as they turned the discussion to various financial matters. The intimidated guard thought he could slip out and was gently—oh, so gently!—sidling toward the door, when Waldorf nailed the beast to the floor with a thundering, "Stay where you are, goat!"

Meanwhile, Rizzo returned and ushered in the usher.

"What's your name?" asked Statler of the plump-faced lady with the periwinkle pigmentation.

"Signora Fiama," she announced in a heavy Italian accent. "But everyone just-a call-a me Mama Fiama. You know me well enough, signori, no? I'm the mother of Johnny Fiama, your star baritone!"

This was said in such a confident tone that, for a moment, Waldorf was impressed. He examined this proud figure, her gray hair pulled into a bun, her faded shawl, old taffeta dress, and shabby shoes. "Well, all right, Mama Fiama, tell me what happened last night to make you and this Clueless character file a report."

"I was-a just thinking about you two signori and wanting to talk-a to you about the *fantasma* so that you might not go through the same troubles as signor Grosse. He wouldn't hear me, either—at first."

"I'm not asking you about all that," said Waldorf. "I'm asking what happened last night."

Mama Fiama turned practically purple with indignation. Never had she been spoken to like that! She rose as though to go, gathering up the folds of her skirt with dignity. But, changing her mind, she sat down again and said, in a haughty voice: "I'll tell-a you what's-a happen: The *fantasma*, he was annoyed again!"

Thereupon, as Waldorf was on the point of bursting, Statler stepped in to take over the interrogation, since it appeared that Mama Fiama thought it quite natural that a voice should be heard to say that a box was occupied when there was nobody in the box.

She was unable to explain this phenomenon, which was old hat to her, except by chalking it up to the Phantom. Nobody, she said, could *see* the ghost in his box, but everybody could *hear* him. She often had, she continued, and she said they could believe her, for she always spoke the truth. "You go and ask-a signor Grosse—ask-a anybody who know me."

Statler said, "Have you actually spoken to the Phantom?"

"As I'm-a speaking to you now, good sir," Mama Fiama replied.

"And when the ghost speaks to you, what does he say?"

"Well, he tell-a me to bring him the baked ziti."

This time, Statler and the others burst out laughing. (Clueless, propped upright in a corner, did nothing, for he had dozed off to sleep.) Statler composed himself and continued. "And how exactly did the Phantom come to ask you for baked ziti?"

"Whenever the *fantasma* visited, he ask-a me for the homemade pastas and pizzas. He has the voice of a *ragazzo*, oh, such a lovely man's voice, and that English accent kinda make-a me swoon! The first time I hear-a three little taps from the inside of the door of Box Five, it was in the middle of the first act. I open the door, listen, look: nobody! And then I hear-a this voice, he say, 'Mama Fiama, bring me some of your superb home cooking, if you please? Maybe a pizza?' It give-a me, how you say, the heebie and the jeebies at first. But the voice went on: 'Don't be frightened, Mama Fiama, I'm the Phantom of the Opera, and I mean you no harm.' And the voice, so soft and kind, seem-a to be sitting in the corner chair, on the right, in the front row."

"And what did you do?"

"Well, you better believe I bring-a the pizzas—*due* pies!" she said, holding up two bony digits.

The eyes of the managers traveled from Mama Fiama to the dozing goat and then to Rizzo, who, standing behind the box keeper, tapped his temple with a finger to convey his opinion that she was most certainly out of her ever-loving gourd.

Meanwhile, the lady went on about her ghost, now praising his generosity. "At the end of the performance, he always give-a me two francs, sometimes five, sometimes even a Starbucks gift card after a long absence. I do love-a those caramel Frappuccinos. I find the gifts on the little shelf. Only, since people have begun to annoy him again, he leave-a me nothing at all . . ."

Statler had heard his fill. "That's enough of the pouty face, Mama Fiama. You can go now."

She nodded. "One night you should come over to my *casa* for the *zuppa di pesce*. You like-a the *zuppa*? I make-a the best in Paris."

From the doorway, Pepé popped his head into the office. "You know, I'm not sure how I feel about the Italian accent, okay. It feel-a little like a stereotype, no?"

Ever accommodating, Mama Fiama asked the prawn, "What is this 'stereotype' you talk of? I don't know it, but if you give-a me the recipe, I make-a for you!"

When Mama Fiama had said her goodbyes and departed, Waldorf and Statler agreed that they would dispense with that old madwoman's services right away.

"Clueless!" called Waldorf, startling the narcoleptic security guard awake. "How do you keep a moron in suspense?"

"Um, I dunno," said Clueless. "How?"

"I'll tell you tomorrow." When the goat had gone, the managers instructed Rizzo to put *him* out to pasture, too. Left alone, the managers decided to look more closely into that little matter of Box Five themselves . . .

Chapter V

THE HURDY-GURDY IN THE GRAVEYARD

Piggy Daaé, owing to intrigues to which I will return later, did not immediately capitalize on her triumph at the Opera and virtually disappeared from the stage for a time. Kermit tried in vain to meet with her, but she refused time and again. He wrote to her repeatedly, asking to call upon her, but received no replies—until one morning when she sent him the following note[12]:

My dear Vicomte Kermit de Chagny:

Don't fret—I have not forgotten the little froglet who went into the sea to rescue my Jet Ski.

I feel that I must write to you today, when

---

[12] The letter, which forms part of the Great Gonzo's collection, is on pale pink parchment with letterhead that reads "Mademoiselle Piggy Daaé: Hogging the Spotlight Since 1879."

61

I am traveling to Cannes,[13] *on an emotional mission. Tomorrow is the anniversary of the death of my poor piano-playing father, Rowlf, whom you knew and who was very fond of you. He is buried there, with his piano. Well, actually* in *a piano, according to his will.*

But of my destination I will say no more, lest you get the wrong idea that I want you to follow me . . . to the graveyard in front of the little church . . . at the bottom of the slope where we used to play as children . . . beside the road where, when we were a little bigger, we said goodbye for the last time.

I only wish I could be more specific, mon ami *(latitude: 43° 33' 10.2564" N, longitude: 7° 1' 2.5284" E).*

It would be perilous for you to come. Definitely do not follow me.

---

[13] The pronunciation of this town is often debated, but here's a helpful mnemonic: *Cans* are in a six-pack. *Khan* is a *Star Trek* bad guy. *Can* is both the town in the South of France and possibly what you're sitting on as you read this.

Je t'embrasse et bisouxx,
Piggy

But love, like a slacker, knows no boss. So Kermit hurriedly checked a railway schedule, wrote a note for his Scottish butler, Angus MacGregor, to take to his brother, Constantine, and hustled to Montparnasse station—just in time to miss the morning train.

"Fiddlesticks," he cursed.

He spent a dismal day in town, and his mood didn't lift until nightfall, when he caught the evening train. Seated in his compartment, he read Piggy's note over and over, smelling its smudges of what he guessed to be chocolate, recalling the sweet memories of his childhood. He spent the rest of the journey in feverish dreams that began and ended with Piggy (in the middle there was something about having to take a test he forgot to study for).

Day was breaking when he arrived at the Cannes train station. He flagged a carriage to take him . . . *somewhere*. Somewhere to find Piggy. He was trying to formulate a plan. As the carriage pulled to the curb, he noticed its bumper sticker: "Honk if you love peace and quiet."

Once they were on their way, the cabbie—a Mr. Polly Lobster, according to the medallion ID posted on the plexiglass that separated the front seat from the back—

revealed to Kermit that just the night before, he'd actually driven an attractive blond "oinker" from the station to a seaside motel. He said she'd crunched through two bags of potato chips on the way. And that was all the evidence Kermit needed to request that the lobster take him to the same destination. The nearer Kermit drew to her, the more fondly he remembered a certain story.

There was once, in a little town outside of Uppsala,[14] a shaggy brown peasant dog with floppy ears named Rowlf, who lived there with his family, digging in the earth by day and playing piano at Sigrid's Swedish Fish Shack by night.

He was a boffo ivory tickler. Not a musician throughout the length and breadth of Scandinavia handled the keys as he did. He had a little daughter (can you guess who?) to whom he taught the musical alphabet before she even knew how to read. (Good guess!)

Tragically, Rowlf's wife passed away in a freak scratch-off lotto accident when little Piggy was just turning six. After that, Rowlf—who focused only on his daughter, his music, and a chew toy shaped like a tuning fork—sold the family doghouse and made the move into Uppsala with a list of the things he thought would best improve their lot in life. That list included:

---

[14] Sweden's fourth-largest city (it wasn't Gothenburg, but it wasn't bad).

1. fame

and

2. fortune.

But the only thing he found was poverty, which had not been on his list at all, so he stopped writing lists altogether. (And, anyway, he couldn't afford pen and paper.)

Living in poverty was a serious drag, so he returned to the suburbs, where he got a gig at the local Renaissance faire. He played his Scandinavian melodies and the lesser-known songs of ABBA, while his little girl, who never left his side, sang along.

One day at the faire, the ogre Professor Sweetums Valérius—a highly regarded, wildly hairy early-modern-period cosplayer—heard them perform and was struck by their talent. He maintained that Rowlf was the best pianist in the world and that Rowlf's daughter, Piggy, had the makings of a great artist. Considering Sweetums's imposing size, no one disagreed. He persuaded them to come with him to Gothenburg.[15]

There, Sweetums generously paid for Piggy's education and instruction. She made rapid progress and charmed everybody with her angelic pipes, her knack for

---

[15] Sweden's second-largest city (it wasn't Stockholm, but it was another step in the right direction).

putting together a look, and her impressive karate skills.

Eventually Sweetums and his wife, the very well-mannered and very, well, magenta Mildred Huxtetter, went to settle in France, and they brought Rowlf and little Piggy with them. Mildred eyed Piggy lovingly through her cat-eye frames and treated the young girl as her own daughter.

But poor Rowlf: In Paris he began to pine away with homesickness. He basically shut himself in with Piggy and the piano, practicing and singing.

Piggy longed to go out and see the city. She had a real affinity for all things French: french fries, French toast, French onion dip with French bread—you get the idea.

Rowlf finally regained some strength in the summer, when the whole family went to stay at the seaside town of Cannes. A lover of digging, he made a piano-size, piano-shaped piano sand castle on the beach and pretended that the sea stopped its roaring to listen to him pound out songs on the keys. But his sandy fantasy only crumbled, not unlike his own ambitions for eking out a life as an artist.

Oblivious to all of this, Piggy tooled around on a Jet Ski in the surf, singing happily at the top of her lungs. Nearby, a little frog made his governess linger at the beach longer than intended, for the frog could not tear himself away from listening to the pure, sweet voice that bound him to Piggy. But a rogue wave suddenly pummeled the pig, knocking her off the Jet Ski. She gave a yell and reached for it, but the watercraft was already far away on the waves.

She heard a voice shout, "Good grief!" and saw a lanky little frog running into the sea, promising, "Don't you worry, I'll fetch your Jet Ski!" And indeed he did. Piggy laughed merrily and hugged the frog, who was (you guessed it again!) none other than young Vicomte Kermit de Chagny, who had been staying at Cannes with an aunt and his brother, Constantine.

Summer lovin' happened so fast.

Piggy and Kermit played together almost every day. Rowlf even gave the young viscount piano lessons, and Kermit quickly perfected "Froggie Went a Courtin'." In this way, Kermit learned to love the same cultured airs that had charmed Piggy's childhood.

Their great treat was when, in the twilight, after the sun had set in the sea, Rowlf would sit with them on the heath and spin one of his fantastic yarns in a low voice. And the moment he stopped, the youngsters would plead for more.

There was one favorite story that began: "A tale as old as time, true as it can be, out beyond Pluto on the planet Koozebane, there was a space creature that loved music more than anything in the universe . . ." The Koozebanian of Music played a part in many of Rowlf's tales. This alien's passion was to inspire others and share its musical secrets, a muse and a mentor rolled into one.

Rowlf maintained that every great musical artist received a visit from the Koozebanian at least once in their life. No one ever sees the Koozebanian, said the wise dog, but it is heard by those who are meant to hear it. And the chosen cannot touch an instrument or open their mouths to sing without producing sounds that put all other sounds to shame. Then people who do not know that the Koozebanian has visited those persons say that they have "genius."

Young Piggy asked her father if *he* had heard the Koozebanian of Music. Rowlf shook his head and said, "Not me." But his eyes lit up as he said, "*You* will hear it one day, my little Piggy! When I blast off this Earth, I'll send it back to you!"

Rowlf was beginning to cough at that time. And you know what that means . . .

Some years later, the young frog, now in his teens, sought out Piggy in Paris. Professor Sweetums had passed away in a freak funicular accident, and Mildred Huxtetter, his widow, now oversaw the abode that housed

Rowlf, Piggy, and Mildred's beloved pet cats, which now numbered seven.

Kermit rang the doorbell, and Rowlf, who was looking quite old and mangy, opened it. Perky Piggy stood behind him with a bag of Bugles. She flushed at the sight of Kermit, asked him a few polite questions, then scarfed down the snacks and ran into the garden, where she took refuge on a bench, prey to feelings that stirred inside her.

Kermit followed her, and they talked shyly till evening. They were quite changed, cautious as two diplomats, and told each other things that had nothing to do with their blossoming sentiments.

"Did you know that the tongue of a blue whale weighs about as much as an elephant?" asked Piggy.

"No," replied Kermit, "but did you know a group of ferrets is called a business?" Nervous Piggy shook her head.

When they took leave of each other by the roadside, Kermit, pressing a kiss on her trembling hand, said, "Oh me, oh my. I will never forget you, Mademoiselle Piggy!" And off he went.

Piggy was pained. She felt she could never be the wife of the Vicomte de Chagny. Their places in society were just too different. To the world at large, he was nobility, she was breakfast.

The young singer tried not to think of Kermit at all and instead devoted herself wholly to her art. She made wonderful progress, and those who subscribed to her YouTube channel prophesied that she would be the greatest vocalist in the world. Meanwhile, Rowlf died (it actually wasn't the cough that got him, it was a freak dung-beetle accident), and Piggy was crushed. She seemed to have lost, with him, her voice and her soul.

She retained just, but only *just*, enough talent to enter the Conservatoire de Paris, where she nearly flunked out, attending classes without enthusiasm and only to please old Mildred Huxtetter, whose few joys in life were Piggy and her pet cats, now sixteen in number.

The first time that Kermit happened to see Piggy performing at the Opera, he was once again struck by her Reubenesque[16] beauty and by the sweet images of the past that it evoked, but he was rather surprised at how, well, *blah* her singing was. He sneaked backstage and secretly followed her around in the wings. More than once, he trailed behind her to the door of her dressing room without her noticing. She seemed, for that matter, to see nobody except the autograph hounds and paparazzi. To everyone else, she was all indifference.

---

[16] No, that's not misspelled. She actually got her figure primarily from Reuben sandwiches.

And then came the lightning flash of the gala performance, when she sang "Manha Manha" and utterly captured Kermit's heart.

And then . . . there was that voice behind the dressing-room door—*"That is a gift that I treasure!"*—and yet no one in the room . . .

Kermit was perplexed. Why didn't she respond when he reminded her of the incident of the Jet Ski? Why did she not recognize him? Why had she ceased performing? Why had she avoided him? And why did she finally write him, only to tell him to forget her?

So many question marks, so little copyediting.

Kermit's cab reached Cannes at last. He paid Polly (and tipped him a much-appreciated cracker) then walked into the motel lobby. And—whattaya know—there she was: Piggy stood before him in a violet jumpsuit, sun visor, and sporty cork wedges.

Kermit suddenly had a frog in his throat. When he found his voice, he revealed all. "I, uh, have feelings for you, Piggy. I'm not sure I can live without you!"

She blushed and turned away. *"Moi?"*

"You knew your letter would make me hop on the train to get here lickety-split. How can you have thought that if you didn't already know I cared for you?"

"It's just that you showing up in my dressing room

the other evening reminded me of long ago and made me write to you as the little piglet that I was then . . ."

"But when you saw me in your dressing room," he ventured, "was that the first time you noticed me?"

She was an excellent fibber, but she decided to tell him the truth. "No," she said, "I had seen you several times in your brother Constantine's box."

"I thought so!" said Kermit, compressing his lips. "But then, when I reminded you that I was the one who had rescued your Jet Ski from the sea, why did you answer like you didn't know me?" The tone of these questions was so rough that she stared at Kermit without replying. He was inwardly aghast at how he seemed to be picking a fight with her, but he was unable to stop. "It was because there was someone in the room with you, Piggy, and you didn't want to let on to him that you could be interested in anyone else!"

"If anyone was in my way that evening," Piggy broke in coldly, "it was *you*! Didn't I tell you to scram?!"

"That's right! So you could stay with Mr. British Accent! The one you told, 'Tonight I gave you my soul' and yadda yadda yadda!"

Piggy grabbed Kermit's arm and clutched it with a strength that no one would have suspected in so frail a creature. (JK! Everyone knew she had a grip like a jackhammer operator.) She asked, "Were you listening outside the door?"

"Yes, I was, and I heard *everything*."

At these words, a deathly pallor spread over Piggy's formerly pink face. She seemed on the point of swooning. Then she turned and bolted to her room.

Kermit was at his wit's end. He watched bitterly as the hours, which he had hoped to find so sweet, slipped past without the presence of the young Swedish songstress. Why did she not come to roam with him along the beach where they had played Pro Kadima in the surf?

Dejected, Kermit went for a walk and found himself in the cemetery. He strolled alone among the gravestones, peering at the inscriptions. One read "I told you I was sick." The next bore the phrase "I knew this would happen." A third proclaimed "Jeez, I was hoping for a pyramid."

When he reached the foot of Rowlf's piano-shaped mausoleum, Kermit respectfully placed a Milk-Bone on the stone. He climbed the slope and sat down on the edge of the heath overlooking the sea. He was surrounded by icy darkness but didn't feel the cold. It was here, he remembered, that he used to sit with little Piggy listening to Rowlf's stories. He smiled at the thought.

Suddenly a voice behind him said, "Do you remember

the legend of the Koozebanian of Music?" It was her. "I have decided to tell you something *très* serious," she began, sitting next to him. "It was on this very spot that my father said, 'When I'm gone, I will send him to you.' Well, Kermie, my father is gone, and *moi* has been visited by the Koozebanian of Music. He comes every day to my dressing room to give me my lessons. And I'm not the only one who's heard him."

"Who else, Piggy?"

"*Vous*, dummy."

"*I've* heard the Koozebanian of Music?"

"When you were listening outside the door! Imagine how shocked I was when you told me that you could hear him, too. And if you had opened the door, you would have seen that there was nobody there!"

Kermit burst out laughing.

Piggy's eyes flashed fire. "You think you heard someone *actually in the room with me*, I suppose?"

"Well . . . ," began the frog, who was growing confused. "That is true . . . I did open the door when you were gone and didn't find anyone there. Piggy, I'm sorry to say it, but I think somebody may be messing with your head."

"Harumph," she huffed, and before he could say another word, she ran off.

Kermit returned to the motel feeling totally down in the dumps. He was told that Piggy had gone to her room immediately after returning. He was staying in the next room over, and he could hear no noise through their adjoining wall.

He ordered Chinese takeout and ate alone, feeling glum. He cracked open the fortune cookie when he had finished. It read: "You will be hungry again in one hour." And he was.

Time passed slowly. It was about half past eleven when he heard someone moving next door. (Piggy did not tread lightly.) She hadn't gone to bed! His heart thumped when he heard her door open slowly on its hinges. Where could she be going, at this hour, when everyone was fast asleep? Of course he had to follow . . .

. . . and the next morning, the young frog was brought back half-frozen, more dead than alive, having been found unconscious in the graveyard. When he finally opened his eyes, he saw Piggy's pleasingly plump face leaning over him.

A few weeks later, the ensuing intrigues at the Opera brought about the intervention of Monsieur Fozzie Bear, an ursine police inspector who was also an aspiring comedian. He interrogated the Vicomte Kermit de Chagny, touching on the curious events of the night in the Cannes cemetery.

Here I quote the questions and answers as given in the official report, starting on page 150:

Q: Hiya! I say I say I say, good evening, ladies and gentlemen!

A: Um, it's just us in the room, Monsieur Bear.

Q: Aww, you can call me Fozzie. And what a lovely crowd we have here tonight!

A: We're alone.

Q: It's called creative visualization. And in my line of work, you have to take advantage of any chance to try out new material in front of an audience.

A: I thought you were a policeman.

Q: Policeman by day, stand-up comic by night— and sometimes a little hoarse in the morning. *Ba-dum-PUM!* Everyone, give yourselves a hand! So, a priest, a rabbi, and a starfish walk into a bar—

A: Uh, aren't you supposed to be asking me questions about what happened at Cannes?

Q: Oh right, yessiree, I can do that. Monsieur Kermit, you say you went to the graveyard?
A: Uh, yes, that's right.

Q: Was it in the *dead* center of town? No but seriously, folks, how'd you get there?
A: I was just following Piggy. Piggy Daaé. She was in a pretty big hurry. I mean, she didn't even stop when she passed a waffle cart.

Q: Annnnd speaking of *grammar*—
A: Grammar? Huh?

Q: Did you hear about the tombstone with the spelling mistake? It was stark *graving* mad!
A: Wow, okay, I think that one could use a little work.

Q: How about this one: You know where gravediggers get their coffee? The burial grounds! No? How about: Why didn't the skeleton go to prom? He had no body to go with! How'm I doing?

A: I suppose you're doing fine, if you have no interest in police work.

Q: Well, between you and me, I really don't, but I gotta pay the rent somehow. Okay, I'll focus. Gimme another chance. Let me just check my notes . . . Here we are. Were you and Mademoiselle Piggy alone in the churchyard?

A: I didn't see anyone else. And it was a full moon, so you could see everything.

Q: Speaking of full moons, you know what happened to the werewolf who swallowed a clock?

A: I have a hunch you're going to tell me.

Q: He got ticks!

A: Should have seen that one coming.

Q: Did you hear anything around you? Because whenever I'm in a cemetery . . . there is always a lot of coffin! Wocka wocka! Halloween humor is one of my fortes. I'm so good at it, it's scary. So what happened next?

A: Well, Piggy knelt down by her father Rowlf's

mausoleum, which is shaped like a baby grand and is as big as one, too. The clock in the church tower began to strike midnight, and on the last bell, I saw Piggy look up and stretch her arms out to the sky. I couldn't figure out for the life of me what she was doing till I heard it: the song "Stairway to Heaven," played on an instrument I later found out was called a hurdy-gurdy.

Q: That's a new one to me.

A: You crank a wheel which rubs like a violin bow against some strings inside, and press keys to change the tone. It sounds like the bagpipe's kooky cousin. Piggy and I knew that song. We'd heard it so much when we were kids. It was Rowlf's favorite tune. When the song stopped, Piggy walked back out the cemetery gate, but I was distracted by a noise from behind the mausoleum.

Q: The hurdy-gurdy player!

A: Yes! I thought the same thing and ran around to the back only to see a shadow slipping into the door of the church. I was quick, though, and managed to catch hold of its blue tail.

Q: Well, well: a clue! So at least we definitely know one thing about him.

A: That he has a blue—

Q: That he is slower than you!

A: Um, gee, I dunno, I think the fact that he has a *blue tail* might be more significant?

Q: Agree to disagree. So what happened next?

A: The shadow turned around, and I saw . . .

Q: Was it that horrible?

A: Well, it certainly was . . . surprising. It darted a look at me from a pair of scorching-green eyes. The rest of its face was in darkness, but I'll never forget those eyes . . . and I don't remember anything else until I woke up at the motel.

Q: Aaaaah! That reminds me of the time a bone doctor and an eye doctor were telling jokes. The bone doctor's jokes were humerus, but the eye doc's jokes were cornea! Wocka wocka!

Chapter VI

STATLER AND WALDORF'S HORRIBLE VISION

We left the managers at the moment they were deciding to look into that little matter of Box Five. And we pick up with them midafternoon, standing in the front row of the theater, their backs to the stage, staring out over the house and up at the mysterious balcony.

"See anything?" asked Statler.

"Nope, but I haven't seen much since 1870," said Waldorf.

"Why don't you get glasses?"

"Girls don't make passes at guys who wear glasses."

"A pass? You can't even get one of those at your annual physical."

Actually it was hard to make out the balcony even if you possessed twenty-twenty vision. The theater was exceedingly dim, and the faraway boxes were curtained on either side with heavy red velvet.

The two managers were almost alone in the huge,

gloomy house—or so they thought. Most of the penguins had gone for a break in the wooden pools of water they kept in the wings. The wan glow of a few candles placed at the lip of the stage made everything take on a creepy, sinister shape. In the orchestra area, a canvas dustcloth covered the rows of seats and appeared to be an angry sea whose waves had been suddenly frozen mid-roil. Statler and Waldorf were the shipwrecked mariners, and the massive unlit chandelier made for an ominous cloud hovering above the dangerous waters. What unknown currents threatened to carry them off? What fearsome creatures swam about under the whitecaps, unseen?

The gents stared silently up at the much-discussed Box Five and pondered why anyone would extend an ocean metaphor quite that far.

Statler wrote about the occasion in his memoirs[17]:

This silly talk about the Phantom of the Opera had no doubt toyed with my mind. Maybe it was the spooky surroundings. Maybe it was the complete silence. Maybe it was the gout. Whatever the reason, we both stood wide-eyed as we saw a shape rising into view up in the box.

---

[17] Not one to be outdone, Waldorf strived to match Statler's introspective outpourings in his own published diaries, collectively titled *Looking Down on Life: My View from the Balcony.*

We stood without moving, trying to make out the vague figure. Suddenly it shifted! There actually was *something* there! Something horrible! It was small and scrawny with a frightful shock of hair on its tiny head, and it had multiple appendages, which it slowly lifted up and down, a horrible vision. Then it opened its terrible mouth and let out a frightful moan—

"BOOOOOOOOOoooooooooOOOOOoooo . . . okay."

Pepé. Of course. It was Pepé the king prawn, the stage manager. He broke into a laugh, then sang out from the balcony, with arms aloft, "Don't cry for me, Argentina!"

Perturbed, Waldorf yelled, "Clam up, shrimp!"

"Sí, Señor Waldorf, I clam up," Pepé called out, "but while I like the way joo are playing on the words, joo would be good to know that a prawn ees not exactly a shrimp."

"It's all the same in tartar sauce, Peps," Waldorf shot back.

"Blame la rata! Rizzo gave me the dare! He bet me half a kilo of the planktons to play the joke. Me, I love the planktons too much, okay, so it was impossible to turn down."

Of course with Statler and me being jokers ourselves, we couldn't stay mad for more than a minute. By the time we made our way up to the box, we were in a cheerful mood and congratulated Pepé on getting us good.

"Now, we've got to end all this distracting speculation

about the magic in Box Five," I announced. I had Rizzo join us to make notes as we took inventory.

In my zeal to find as many relevant documents as possible, I discovered Rizzo's jottings from that day inside the tiny notebook he carried in his pocket. Here's what the rat wrote:

THE CURTAINS—Ya got yer red velvet drapes hangin' on either side a' the box. I think they're kinda tacky, but the high-falutin' folks go for these sorta trappings. Personally, curtains ain't my thing—too wet for 'em in the sewer colony where I live in Brooklyn. (You never heard of a Brooklyn in Paris? It's in the 21st arrondissement.)

THE LEDGE—There's a shelf where the people watching the opera can put their programs and gloves and binoculars or what have ya. No trick levers or secret buttons we could find. Though I did note a smear of spilled Alfredo sauce. (Yeah, I tasted it. Not bad, but coulda used a little more Parmesan.)

THE CARPET—We searched all around the floor to see if there were hidden trapdoors or anything dodgy but only found some sticky stale Jujubes (ate 'em), a humongous hairball (saved it for my nest), and six fingernail clippings. (Nail clippings! And people think rats *are disgusting?)*

THE FURNITURE—The box has got six sorta crummy armchairs. I'd told Grosse it was time to renovate this joint. "Just tack on a few francs to the ticket price for a 'theater restoration charge,'" I says to him. "The Shuberts get away with it." But nah, he didn't listen. Anyways, we found nuttin', even in the chair where people say they heard the ghost's voice. My theory? It was probably the intermission cocktails talking, if ya get my drift . . .

Chapter VII

THE *FAUST* AND THE FURIOUS

When they reached their office on Saturday morning, the managers found a letter from the Phantom worded in these terms:

> *So you're declaring war between us? If better sense should prevail and you still hold out hope for peace, here is my ultimatum. It consists of the three following conditions:*
>
> *#1.—You must give me back sole use of my private box, and I wish it to be at my free disposal henceforward.*
> *B.—The part of Margarita shall not be sung as usual by Yolanda this evening but by Piggy Daaé. Never mind about Yolanda—she will be ill.*
> *III.—I absolutely insist upon the loyal services of Mama Fiama, my box keeper, whom you will*

reinstate in her functions forthwith.

Let me know by a letter handed directly to Mama Fiama, who will personally see that it reaches me, that you accept, as your predecessor J.P. Grosse did, the conditions in my memorandum book relating to my monthly allowance. I will inform you later how you are to pay it to me.

If you refuse, you will present a performance tonight in a house with a curse upon it—a curse, I say! Mwah hah haaahhhh! (The medium of print is not ideal for conveying how impressive that menacing laugh actually is.)

Heed my warning!
The Phantom.

"I've had just about enough of this twaddle," shouted Waldorf, bringing his fists down on his desk. "Ouch."

Just then, the business manager, Sam Eagle, entered. "Good morning, gentlemen. Jacques Roach is outside and would like to see you."

"And just what is a Jacques Roach?" asked Waldorf.

"He's our stable keeper."

"Stables? We're an opera house, not a racetrack!" Waldorf looked at Statler. "Did you know we had horses?"

"No, but after seeing some of our shows, I knew we had dogs!"

"We need trained horses for the processions in certain operas," explained Sam patiently. "The audience eats it up. We have twelve of them—actually, eleven horses and one camel—and it is Jacques's business to train the beasts."

Just then the multi-legged Jacques Roach himself scampered in, carrying a tiny riding whip. "My dear managers, I have come to ask you to sack the whole stable."

"I agree," asserted Statler. "We should definitely get rid of those animals."

"I'm not talking about the animals," he hissed, "I'm talking about the stablemen."

Waldorf shot a look at Sam. "We have *stablemen*, too?"

"Six of them," said Jacques.

"That's expensive," exclaimed Waldorf.

Statler nodded in agreement, adding, "We shouldn't need more than four stablemen for twelve beasts."

"Eleven," said Jacques.

"Twelve," said Statler.

"Eleven," said Jacques.

"All right, you two," said Sam.

"Fore!" said Waldorf, practicing a golf swing.

"Let me explain. We *did* have twelve, but now it's only eleven, since the camel, Sopwith, was stolen," Jacques clarified with an irritated crack of his tiny whip. "Me? I was no fan. That camel spits more than a shortstop in extra innings. But somebody's got to be held accountable for letting the Phantom take him."

"The Phantom?!" the two old men said in tandem.

"Well, yes, who *wouldn't* think that after seeing a dragon-shaped shadow riding a two-humped camel! I spied them disappearing into the darkness of the underground cellars."

Waldorf stood. "I think I've heard enough. You can bet we'll find that camel-thieving Phantom and give him an earful. Now be gone and stop bugging us."

Roach gave one more dramatic whip crack then bowed and withdrew.

When they were alone again, a furious Waldorf glared at Sam and said, "Send that idiot insect packing."

"But—"

"No buts, Sam. If his nutty claims of a galloping ghost get out, people will laugh and make fun of us."

Statler raised his bushy gray brows. "More than they

already do?" At that moment the door opened, and Mama Fiama rushed in, holding a letter in one hand and a plate of tiramisu in the other. Flustered, she addressed the managers. "Excuse-a me, signori, but I get a letter this morning, from the Phantom? He tell-a me to come to you, that you had something for me to give-a to him." She held up the plate of tiramisu. "Luckily, I just finish making this-a little treat I could bring for him so—"

She didn't have a chance to complete the sentence. She saw livid Waldorf's face, and he was about ready to burst. First, his left arm seized upon her quaint person and sent her in so unexpected a semicircle that she uttered a little yelp. Next, his right foot imprinted its sole on the backside of her black taffeta skirt, which certainly had never before undergone a similar outrage in a similar place, and the tiramisu went flying into the air. The lady looked up in surprise as the airborne dessert reached maximum height and then made its rapid descent—right onto her face.

It happened so quickly that Mama Fiama, when back outside in the passage with Rizzo, was still quite bewildered and seemed not to understand. A clump of tiramisu slid from her cheek and hit the floor. The rat took a taste. "Not bad, but could use just a touch more nutmeg," he said, smacking his lips.

Finally, the usher snapped back to her senses, and the Opera rang with her indignant yells.

About the same time, Yolanda, who had a ritzy town house in the rue du Faubourg Saint-Honoré, was reading her fan mail and having breakfast in bed from a tray on her lap. Among the notes was an anonymous missive, written in red ink, which read:

> *If you perform tonight, be prepared for a great misfortune the moment you open your mouth to sing, a misfortune worse than . . .* a really irritating paper cut! *No, it'll be like something even more intense. A misfortune worse than . . .* a Slurpee brain freeze! *No, that's not bad enough. We need some big stakes here. Worse than . . . worse than . . . Aha, how about, worse than . . .* death! *Yes, a misfortune* WORSE THAN DEATH! *Mwah hah haaahhhh! (Drat—so underwhelming. I can't wait until they invent recording devices.)*

The letter took away Yolanda's appetite. She turned over her tray with a crash and bellowed, "Bean Bunny!" Her personal assistant, an impossibly cute little rabbit with a blush-pink nose and eyes like two chocolate hard candies, hopped into action, appearing at the foot of her bed. "Yes, Yolanda?"

"The haters are back. Look at this letter," she said with a snarl. "Isn't the first, won't be the last."

"But it's only one letter," ventured Bean Bunny, affecting an adorably peppy expression after he scanned it. Everyone found him irresistible—everyone but his employer, that is. Yolanda was impervious to his charms, which only made him try all the harder. "Why not take that frown and turn it upside—"

"Aw, put a cork in it, carrot breath. I don't need yer cheerleader routine right now. And don't tell me I'm overreacting. There are thousands of jealous Janes out there, *thousands*, I tell ya, and they all wanna see me flop. Wicked plots are being hatched every day. Conspiracies so big, they'd shock WikiLeaks! But Yolanda is one tough rat, and I ain't gonna be intimidated, ya hear me?!"

He heard her. At that volume, the whole arrondissement heard her.

The truth is that if there was a conspiracy, it was led by Yolanda herself against poor Piggy, who had no suspicion of it. Yolanda had never forgiven Piggy for the triumph the younger singer had achieved when taking her place at a moment's notice to perform "Mahna Mahna."

When Yolanda heard of the astounding reception bestowed upon her understudy, she was at once cured of a bad case of sulking against the management, who'd uncharacteristically sent her an insulting note earlier in the day, written in a very peculiar red ink, that prompted her to retaliate by calling in sick for the gala. But after Piggy's tour de force, she'd lost the slightest inclination to ever play hooky again.

From that time, she had worked with all her might to get even, enlisting the services of influential friends to persuade Statler and Waldorf not to give Piggy an opportunity for a fresh triumph. "As my dear mother always taught me," she had explained to Bean Bunny, "if you can't say something nice about someone, say it behind their back." And true to that instruction, the celebrated but heartless diva made the most scandalous remarks about Piggy at the theater and generally tried to cause her trouble whenever she could.

"So what are you going to do?" asked the rabbit with trepidation as he passed the threatening letter back to Yolanda. He rested his chin sweetly on his paws and fluttered his eyelashes.

Oblivious to his awww-inspiring expression, she corrected him: "What am *I* gonna do? What are *we* gonna do."

"We?!" He recoiled. "You're not going to make me do bad things again . . . are you?"

"*Good* and *bad* are relative terms. What's bad for Piggy is good for me. And what's good for me is good for you staying on the payroll. Get it?"

"Got it."

"*Good.* So what you're gonna do, sweetcheeks, is spread the word that Piggy's plotting to sabotage me at tonight's performance. Tell all my pals that they gotta pack the house and be ready to cheer me—or jeer her—if that porker dares to cross this rat. Now, go on—sashay away!"

It was nearly five o'clock when Bean Bunny returned to Yolanda's flat after hopping around Paris, spreading the message to all her friends. He discovered a note slipped under the front door, addressed in the same red ink as the first.

Bean gingerly brought it to his boss. The note was short but not sweet:

> *Now hear this, vermin: You have a frightful cold. If you are smart, you will see that it is a terribly unwise idea to try to sing tonight. Don't set foot on that stage or you'll be sorry.* 😠😒👉😣😿😾

Bean Bunny read over her shoulder. "Ooo, pretty pictures."

Yolanda sneered, smoothed her famously fetching whiskers with her paws, and sang a scale of la-la-las to reassure herself. "How did that sound to you, Bean?"

"Fine."

"Fine?"

"Good."

"Good?"

"Um . . . amazing?"

"That's more like it."

Her friends were faithful to their promise and packed the audience that night. But they looked around in vain for the fierce conspirators whom they were supposed to suppress. The only unusual thing was the presence of Statler and Waldorf sitting in Box Five, which was not their usual box.

Sam Eagle's amplified voice suddenly boomed throughout the theater. "Mesdames and messieurs, for the safety of the performers, and just out of good manners, respect, and decency, we ask that during the show you refrain from taking daguerreotypes. Merci, and God bless America! And France."

"Lucky for me," Statler boasted to Waldorf, "I have a photographic memory."

His partner raised an eyebrow. "Too bad you ran out of film a few decades back!"

In the pit, the musicians readied to start. The Opera featured an all-vegetable orchestra: string beans on violins and cellos; beets on drums and snap peas on percussion; and finally, fiddlehead ferns on flügelhorn (they all went against their stringing upbringing and learned to play the brass).

Lew Zealand, the eccentric conductor, raised the fish he used in place of the typical baton and began to count out the musical measures. An artist of great feeling, he really put his sole into his work.

Up went the curtain. Johnny Fiama played the lead role of Dr. Faust, an aging scholar who makes a deal with the devil to regain his youth.[18] He had hardly finished the character's first appeal to the powers of darkness when Waldorf, who was sitting in the Phantom's supposed favorite seat—the front chair on the right—leaned over to Statler and asked, "Has the Phantom whispered anything in your ear yet?"

"Eh?" replied Statler, turning his other ear to Waldorf.

"Oh, is that your better side?"

---

[18] *Faust*, a five-act grand opera, is by Charles Gounod with a French libretto by Jules Barbier and Michel Carré. It is loosely based on *Faust, Part I*, by Johann Wolfgang von Goethe. Goethe's lesser-known follow-up, *2 Faust 2 Furious*, focused on a man who made a deal with the diesel.

"What's that you say? You see butterflies? You should get your eyes checked."

"You old fool, can't you hear?"

"*Beer?* No, no beer for me. It puts me to sleep—and with Johnny Fiama onstage, I won't need any help with that!"

The first act passed without incident, which did not surprise Yolanda's friends, since her character, Margarita, didn't sing in this act. As for the managers, they looked at each other with relief when the curtain fell. "One down, four to go!" said Statler.

"Looks like the ghost is tardy to the party," said Waldorf.

The door of the box suddenly opened, and in rushed Pepé. The old men were amazed to see the stage manager there at such a time, when he was normally busy backstage.

"*Ay caramba*, do I got some scuttlebutt, okay. Everyone say that Piggy Daaé's friends ees making the plot against Yolanda."

"A plot?" said Waldorf, knitting his brow.

"Finally!" exclaimed Statler. "That's just what this book's been needing."

"But Pepé think ees Yolanda herself who's up to something!" Just then, the lights went down for the next act. Pepé let out a small shriek and hustled back to his post in the wings.

Statler was surprised. "So Piggy has friends?"

Waldorf pointed across the auditorium.

Statler squinted in the indicated direction. "You mean the tall, skinny orange-haired guy?"

"That's Beaker, one of the stagehands. Sam Eagle promoted him to usher after we fired Mama Fiama. Tonight's his first night. No, Piggy's friends are up there in the Grand Tier, Box Nine."

Statler scrutinized the pair of tuxedoed frogs. "Is that Constantine, the Russian count?"

"He's not really Russian, he just sounds like it."

"And I'm not really interested, I just act like it. Ha ha!"

Waldorf grinned. "You know, Constantine pulled me aside the other day and sang Piggy's praises pretty convincingly."

"Sang convincingly, did he? Then maybe he should be playing Johnny Fiama's part."

"Touché!"

"And who is that young frog beside him? He looks like he's about to toss his cookies."

"That's his younger brother, the viscount Kermit. He's here every night."

"Well then, no wonder he looks ill!" Statler was clearly cheering up fast.

Soon Piggy entered and crossed upstage,[19] playing the character of Siebel, a young man who's in love with Margarita.[20] Yolanda's pals expected to hear her rival greeted with an overwhelming ovation. But to everyone's surprise, nothing happened.

On the other hand, when Yolanda (as Margarita, the object of Faust's attention) vamped across the stage and sang the only two lines allotted her in this second act, she was received with wild applause so unexpected and uncalled for that those not clapping were utterly confused.

A puzzled patron in the audience whispered to Beaker, "Why is everyone so enthusiastic?"

"Meep meep meep," was Beaker's baffled reply.

"I'm impressed with your eloquence," said the patron.

This act also finished without incident, so Team Yolanda was convinced the next act would deliver the slight the rat had predicted. During intermission, the managers

---

[19] Theater novices might find stage directions confusing, but the terms are really very simple to break down: In is down, down is front, out is up, up is back, off is out, on is in, and of course left is right and right is left. See? Easy-peasy!

[20] Siebel is what they call in the theater a "trouser role," which means a female performer portrays a male character. It's also known as a "breeches role," a "pants role," or in a sushi restaurant, a "California role."

left the box to find out more about the plot of which Pepé had spoken but uncovered nothing, so they soon returned, shrugging and deeming the whole affair silly.

But all in Box Five was not as they had left it. The first thing they saw on entering just as the house lights dimmed for the start of the next act was a Starbucks gift card sitting on the little shelf affixed to the ledge. They looked at each other. They had no inclination to laugh. All that Mama Fiama had told them returned to their memory . . . and then . . . and then . . . they seemed to feel a curious sort of draft around them . . .

They sat down in silence.

The scene onstage represented Margarita's garden. As Piggy sang her first two lines, with a bouquet of lilacs in her hand, she raised her head and briefly locked eyes with Kermit in his box. From that moment, her voice seemed less sure, less crystal clear than usual. Something seemed to deaden and dull her singing . . .

"That pig is a hot mess!" whispered one of Yolanda's friends in the audience.

"She's pitchy," said another.

"It's like she's bleating," said Statler.

"Yeah," said Waldorf, "and so are my ears!"

Kermit could tell that Piggy was blowing it. He helplessly hid his head under his hands and cringed.

Beside him, Constantine frowned. Usually so cold and correct, with a certain Russian-style reserve ingrained in him, the count would have to be very angry to betray his inner feelings like that, by outward signs.

And boy oh boy, was he ever angry. He'd watched as his brother's natural optimism had slowly evaporated over the past few weeks after he returned from a rapid and mysterious journey to Cannes in an alarming mental state. The explanation that had followed was unsatisfactory, so the count asked Piggy Daaé for an appointment. She had the audacity to reply that she could not see either him or his brother!

In his box, the count groused under his breath, "я доберусь до сути этого . . ."[21]

Kermit, behind the curtain of his hands, was thinking only of the letter that he received on his return to Paris, where Piggy, fleeing from Cannes like a booed filmmaker, had arrived before him:

My petite grenouille,

> *You must have the courage not to see me*
> *or speak of me again. I know how hard it is*
> *to imagine a life without all my glamour and*

---

[21] Translation from the Cyrillic: "I'll get to the bottom of this . . ."

pizzazz, but if you love me just a little—and really, who doesn't?—then do this for moi, *for* moi *who will never forget* toi, *my dear Kermie-wermie, rescuer of Jet Skis.*

My life depends upon it.

Your life depends upon it.

The fate of all humanity depends on it.

XOXO,
Your little chicharrón

At the bottom of the page was a smudge of something yellow. He sniffed it (*spicy mustard . . . her favorite mustard . . .*) and wept.

In the theater, there were sudden thunders of applause as Yolanda made her entrance to sing her ballad. Thenceforth, certain of herself, certain of her friends in the house, certain of her voice and her success, Yolanda flung herself into her part without restraint of modesty. She sang Margarita's line, "*I feel without alarm . . .*" and then a terrible thing happened: Yolanda went to hit her high note—and *mooed like a cow.*

"Mooooo!"

Time seemed to stop. There was a baffled look on Yolanda's face, confusion on the faces of the audience, shock on the faces of the veggies in the pit.

Lew Zealand was so surprised, he sent his fish flying—it boomeranged an arc around the auditorium and slapped back into his hand.

Everyone felt that Yolanda's blunder was not natural, that there was some spell behind it. Poor despairing, crushed, wretched Yolanda! The uproar in the house was indescribable. Even Bean Bunny felt pity for his berating boss.

After some seconds spent asking herself if she had really heard that infernal noise that issued from her throat, Yolanda tried to persuade herself that it was not so, that she was the victim of some illusion of the ear and not of an act of treachery on the part of her voice.

Meanwhile, in Box Five, Statler and Waldorf had paled. This extraordinary and inexplicable incident had brought on a tinge of dread that was even more mysterious because they had undoubtedly fallen under the direct influence of the Phantom. Yes, they felt that the ghost *was right there*—around them, behind them, beside them. They felt his presence without seeing him; they heard his breath! They were sure that there were *three* souls in the box. They froze . . . They thought of running away . . . They were afraid of falling and breaking a hip . . .

What was going to happen?

This is what happened: Yolanda—bravely, heroically, undoubtedly too cocky for her own good—began to sing again. But oh, what a dreadful idea.

"*I feel without alarm*-mmmoooo! Moooo! Moooo!"

The house broke into a wild tumult. Statler and Waldorf fell back in their chairs and dared not even turn around. They didn't have the strength—*because the ghost was chuckling behind their backs!* They distinctly heard his voice, the mouthless voice, saying: "It seems Yolanda is singing tonight to bring down the chandelier! *Mwah hah haaahhh!*"

They raised their eyes to the ceiling, and what they saw was unbelievable: The immense mass of the chandelier was slipping down at the call of that fiendish voice. Released from its hook, it plunged from the ceiling and came smashing down amid a thousand shouts of terror and a wild rush for the doors.

The next morning, a newspaper appeared with this headline: A PERFORMANCE SO BAD, IT LITERALLY BROUGHT DOWN THE HOUSE. All the papers of the day state that there were a few patrons superficially wounded and one killed. The fatality had occurred when the chandelier plummeted right onto the individual whom Sam had appointed to succeed Mama Fiama—it landed squarely on the unfortunate, orange-capped head of Beaker.[22]

In the audience, all had watched the scene with horror, but one patron in particular witnessed it with a lasting fascination: that was Floyd, an opera aficionado and the bass player for the popular Paris wedding band Electric Mayhem. He was an aspiring musical-theater composer who took significant inspiration from the fixture's dramatic plunge. One day long after, he'd achieve fame far and wide for writing an entertainment that re-created the selfsame moment. In fact, you may know him by his stage name: Andrew Floyd Webber.

---

[22] Beaker was given a proper burial in Père Lachaise, Paris's largest cemetery, the final resting place of Oscar Wilde, Molière, and Jim Morrison. His headstone reads: "Meep Meep RIPeep."

Chapter VIII
IN PURSUIT OF PIGGY

That evening and its immediate aftermath was a downer for everybody. Pepé tasked the penguins with cleaning up the damage, and they gave him the cold shoulder (well, as arctic birds, their shoulders were always cold, but still). Sam Eagle was embroiled with the insurance company, and he got even more grumpy than usual. Yolanda took to her bed, heaping untold abuse on poor Bean Bunny. And Piggy Daaé? She flat out disappeared.

Kermit was the first to notice the prima donna's absence. He wrote to her at her small apartment, where she still lived with her surrogate mother, Mildred Huxtetter, but he got no reply. His grief increased when he nightly attended the opera but never found Piggy's name on the program. The subsequent performances of *Faust*—sparsely attended, since patrons were feeling shaky on the safety issue—were played by Piggy's understudy, Annie Sue, who, despite having a pretty face and a dynamite blond Afro, lacked that ineffable star power that Piggy possessed.

Fozzie Bear's inquest into the chandelier incident had ended in a verdict of accidental death, caused by the wear and tear of the chains by which it was hung from the ceiling.[23] Waldorf and Statler at this time appeared so absentminded, so mysterious, so incomprehensible that many of the subscribers thought that some event even more horrible than the fall of the chandelier must have affected their state of mind.[24]

In their daily encounters, the old coots were even more impatient than usual, except with Mama Fiama, who had been rehired as usher and box keeper. "I told-a you so!" she said, gloating, when they came to her, apologetic, and let her make them spaghetti.

For her, revenge was a dish best served with marinara.

The managers' reception of Kermit, when he came to ask about Piggy, was anything but cordial. They curtly told him that she had requested a leave of absence for health reasons, and they referred him to Dr. Honeydew.

"Did you examine Piggy?" Kermit asked the doctor

---

[23] In Fozzie's official report he wrote: "Clearly the matter of the chandelier *weighs heavily* upon the managers. This was definitely a *chain* reaction. But I don't mean to make *light* of the matter. Wocka wocka!"

[24] And as we now know, they were right . . .

at his lab. "Is she all right?"

"She said she just had a headache. I took her at her word and gave her some acetylsalicylic acid."

"You mean aspirin?"

Honeydew slapped his forehead. "*That's* it! I can never remember the name."

"What else did she say?"

"We didn't talk long. I had to take care of a man who fell into an upholstery machine."

"Oh dear, is he all right?"

"He seems to be recovered."

Kermit left the lab feeling gloomy. He decided to drop in on Mildred Huxtetter, despite clearly remembering the strong phrases in Piggy's letter forbidding him to make any attempt to see her. But what he had witnessed in the graveyard, what he had heard behind the dressing-room door, and his kooky conversation with Piggy at the edge of the moor made him suspect some devilish machination at work.

He trembled as he rang at a little flat in the rue Notre-Dame-des-Victoires. The door was opened by the housekeeper, Lenny Lizard, a reputable reptile that Mildred had hired from Paris's finest all-animal employment agency. He cut a fine figure in a morning coat and formally pleated ascot tie. Kermit asked to speak to Madame Huxtetter. Lenny led the way—Kermit was careful not to tread on his tail—and showed the visitor into a small and scantily furnished drawing room, in which portraits of Professor Sweetums and old Rowlf hung on the wall, along with a poster for the musical *Cats*. Which was appropriate because there were cats everywhere. *Actual* cats, actually *everywhere*: curled up on the chairs, playing with the drapery tassels, winding around the table legs, nestled among novels on the bookshelves.

"Madame asks Monsieur le Vicomte to excuse her," said Lenny. "She can only see him in her bedroom, because she can no longer stand on her poor legs due to a freak flapjack accident, and the cats underfoot make moving about too dangerous."

Kermit cocked his head. "Why not get rid of the cats, then?"

"She doesn't want the fleas to get lonely."

A few minutes later, Kermit was ushered into a dim room where he at once recognized the good, kind, magenta face of Piggy's benefactress. Mildred Huxtetter's hair was now as white as the pearls around her neck, but her eyes had grown no older; never, on the contrary, had their expression been so bright and childlike.

Despite the room being rather warm, a lumpy wool afghan covered the bed. No, scratch that—upon closer inspection, Kermit could see it was a veritable blanket of dozing felines, who, taking minimal notice of the visitor, shifted and stretched, then curled back into sleep.

"Kermit!" Mildred cried gaily, putting out both her hands. Kermit clasped them.

"Madame," Kermit said gently, "where is Piggy?"

"She is with her good genius, the Koozebanian of Music!"

The viscount dropped into a chair, the trio of groggy cats it held wriggling out from under him in the nick of time.

Really? Piggy was with the Koozebanian of Music? Mildred smiled at him and put her finger to her lips, adding, "You must not tell anyone!"

"Oh sure, you can rely on me," Kermit assured her, wondering if she'd gone fully round the bend. He hardly knew what he was saying, for his ideas about Piggy, already greatly confused, were becoming more and more entangled, and it seemed as if everything was beginning to spin around him, around the room, around that kind, cat-covered lady.

He sighed and tried to unravel three things that seemed to be somehow related: the Koozebanian of Music of whom Piggy had spoken to him so strangely; the blue-tailed creature he had seen in the graveyard at Cannes; and the Opera's Phantom, whose fame had come to his ears via a group of penguin sceneshifters who were repeating Beauregard's ghastly description of the ghost.

"You know," said Mildred, "Piggy is very fond of you. She used to speak of you every day."

"Used to . . . ? And what did she say?"

"She told me you made her a proposal!" And the good old lady chortled.

Flushing with embarrassment, Kermit sprang from the chair, accidentally punting a shaggy tabby in the process.

"What's this? Where are you going?" asked Mildred. "Sit down again at once, will you? If you're angry with me for laughing, I beg your pardon. After all, what has happened isn't your fault. Didn't you know? Did you think that Piggy was—oh, how do the kids put it? 'Single and ready to mingle'?"

"Do you mean that she is . . . ," poor Kermit began, almost choking up, "*going steady* with someone?"

"Why no! You know as well as I do that Piggy couldn't, even if she wanted to!"

"But I don't know anything about it! Why couldn't she?"

"Because of the Koozebanian of Music, of course! He forbids her to . . . without forbidding her. You see, if she did, she would never hear him again. He said that he would go away forever! So, you understand, she can't let the Koozebanian of Music go. It's quite natural."

"Good grief. 'Natural' wouldn't be the way I'd describe *any* of this."

"I thought Piggy had told you all that when she met you at Cannes, where she went with her good genius."

"Whoa. She went to Cannes with her good genius?!"

"That is to say, he arranged to meet her there, in the Cannes graveyard, at Rowlf's piano mausoleum. He promised to play her 'Stairway to Heaven' on the hurdy-gurdy!"

Kermit took a deep breath. "Can you please tell me where this genius lives?"

The old lady raised her eyebrows and said, "Why, on planet Koozebane, of course."

Kermit was baffled. He didn't know what to say about an extraterrestrial genius who supposedly beamed down nightly from outer space to haunt the dressing rooms at the Opera.

He tried to connect the dots, realizing the possible state of mind of a pig brought up by a superstitious dog and an obsessive cat lady—oh, the cross-species consequences of it all! Still he wanted more info, so he asked, "How long has she known this genius?"

"It's been about three months since he began to give her lessons."

The viscount threw up his gangly arms in despair.

"And where does the genius give her lessons?"

"Why, in her dressing room. It would be impossible in this little flat."

"Yes, I suppose the neighbors would complain."

"No, the cats would!"

Kermit hurriedly took leave of Mildred and walked in a pitiful state to the home he shared with his brother and their little fluffy white dog, Foo-Foo. Inside, kind Constantine consoled his brother without asking for explanations, and anyway, Kermit wasn't about to tell him the crazy story of the Koozebanian of Music.

His brother suggested they go out in the Marais that evening for mayfly fondue, one of Kermit's favorite treats. Overcome as he was with despair, Kermit would probably have refused any invitation if the count had not, as an inducement, told him that Piggy had been spotted the night before on a street that passed through the Marais.

At first, Kermit refused to believe it, but Constantine told him in such exact detail that he stopped protesting. "She vas seen ridink in carriage with window down," Constantine reported. "Vas big moon shinink in sky. Ohhh, vas her for sure. As for other person in carriage, only shadowy outline was beink seen."

Kermit dressed in frantic haste, blew off his bro, and flagged a cab. As it pulled over to the curb, the driver shouted out the window, "Hey, buddy, I remember you from Cannes a few weeks back!"

Kermit looked up, and sure enough, he recognized the driver as well: It was Polly Lobster. "Hi ho," said Kermit, "but what are you doing in Paris? Isn't Cannes at least a full day's drive from here?"

"Seasonal migration," the lobster explained with a shrug. "Mother Nature's my dispatcher."

Polly zipped him over to the street in question. It was deserted but very bright under the moonlight. Kermit asked the cabbie to wait for him at the corner and, hiding himself as well as he could behind a tree near the road, stood stamping his feet to keep warm. Half an hour or so later, Polly gave a whistle and pointed his claw at a carriage that had turned the corner and was heading in Kermit's direction.

As it approached, he could make out a feminine figure leaning her head from the open window to look at the sky. Oh, he knew that blond hair—though she seemed to be wearing a strange hat with two mounds on top . . .

Suddenly the moon shed a pale gleam over her features.

"Piggy!"

The name had sprung spontaneously from Kermit's heart and his lips, and unfortunately, in the stillness of the night, it startled the horses and made them giddyap. Before he could figure out a plan, the carriage dashed past and was soon no more than a black spot on the white road. He called out again, in vain: *"Piiiiiiiiggy!"*

But alas, the coach was gone.

Heartbroken, and with a lackluster eye, he stared down that desolate street and into the pale, dead night. *Kermit,* he thought, *how that little sly fox of a pig has trifled with you!*

It was then that he noticed something on the pavement. He walked over and picked it up: the hat she had been wearing. Not a hat exactly . . . but a Mickey Mouse beanie? And he realized that this road led directly to and from . . . Disneyland Paris?

While he had been painfully pining away on this emotional roller coaster, she'd been at an amusement park riding *actual* roller coasters!

"Hey, bud," Polly called from the corner, "you want I should keep the meter runnin'?"

"Thanks, Polly, but I'll walk from here."

"You crazy? You'll freeze to death!"

"Only if I'm lucky," said Kermit, dejected.

In the morning, Kermit's butler, the kilt-wearing Angus MacGregor, found him sitting on his bed. It was obvious to the Scotsman that the frog had not slept, and he assumed that was due to some hard partying.

Angus asked, "Did you tie one on last evenin'?"

Kermit slowly shook his head.

"Aye, right. You musta. Were you oot yer nut? Doesn't look like ya kipped at all."

Kermit noticed that the butler had brought in the morning's letters. Instantly recognizing Piggy's pink paper, he grabbed them from the man's hands.

"Yer aff yer heid, ya wee scunner," said a startled Angus, "snatchin' them peipers awa' from me laik that!"

But Kermit had stopped listening. He noticed an orange smudge on the envelope and held it to his nose (*nacho cheese! she loves nacho cheese!*), then read the letter:

Dearest Kermie,

> *Go to the masquerade ball at the Opera on the night after tomorrow. At midnight, be in the little room past the fireplace in the foyer. Stand near the statue of Handel by the door that leads to the Rotunda. Come disguised as Frankenstein. That way* moi *can recognize* toi *even as you walk around the party fully infrognito.*

Till then,
Your petite Piggy

Chapter IX

THE MUSIC AND THE MIRROR

The pink envelope was covered with mud and unstamped. The front bore the words *To be handed to M. le Vicomte Kermit de Chagny*, written in a swirly cursive with hearts dotting each *i*. It must have been flung out the carriage window in the hope that a passerby would pick up the note and deliver it, which was indeed what happened.

Kermit read it over again with fevered eyes, his hope revived. He remembered Piggy's story—how after her father's death she was fed up with everything in life, including her art. She went through the conservatoire like a poor soulless singing machine. And suddenly this bizarro Koozebanian of Music had appeared upon the scene. She sang "Mahna Mahna" and triumphed!

And for three months he had been giving her lessons. Ah, he was an effective teacher, to be sure. But now he was taking her to theme parks! O misery!

Still, he bought the dang costume.

The hour of the meeting came at last. He had donned the Frankenstein neck bolts and the flattop headpiece, stuffed the shoulders of his black suit jacket, and pulled on a pair of chunky black work boots. (Happily, he didn't need to bother with the green makeup.)

The ball was mobbed with members of the Opera company, subscribers, and a paparazzi-worthy cohort of supermodels, rappers, and champion mathletes, the latter of whom, as the evening progressed, began to create a tremendous din (let me tell you, those STEM types are the biggest party animals!).

In full costume, Kermit climbed the grand staircase at five minutes to twelve. It was a total traffic jam. Some numbskull had arranged a bunch of mannequins in an eye-popping array of garish costumes all up and down the stairs. Kermit thought that if this were a musical, here would be a good place for a big ensemble number. But he deemed it a feng shui fail.

Crossing the foyer, he found himself snaking through a mad whirl of dancing couples. As they twirled past, he overheard snippets of their conversations.

"I felt so unlucky on my wedding day," said a lady reveler. "Why?" asked her partner. She replied, "Because I wasn't going to marry the best man!"

As another couple breezed by, one asked the other, "What did you say when you bumped into that dolphin?"

"I told him I didn't do it on porpoise."

And a third duo waltzed into earshot. The man said, "So you're a seamstress? How's business?"

The seamstress shrugged. "Only sew-sew."

Kermit at last reached the room beyond the fireplace mentioned in Piggy's letter. He leaned against a doorframe near the designated statue. "Hi ho, Handel," he said anxiously, then he waited—but not for long.

Across the room, he spied a towering dark wig with a lightning bolt of white zigzagging from each temple. It bobbed toward him above the heads of the costumed crowd. Soon the rest of the individual came into view: She wore a loose-fitting floor-length white shift, her skin paled with powder. Clever, clever Piggy: She was dressed as the Bride of Frankenstein, and Kermit's heart jumped a little at the seeming significance.

The Bride spied him and raised her finger to her lips. He understood and followed her in silence.

As they passed through the great foyer, Kermit could not help noticing a figure dressed in full football regalia, including shoulder pads and a helmet with an intricate face mask that in the dim light rendered the wearer's visage impossible to make out. As Kermit neared, the footballer turned in his direction, and *its eyes glowed green*. Kermit knew instantly: It was the creature from the graveyard in Cannes!

Piggy caught Kermit by the arm and dragged him from the foyer, far from the mad crowd through which the ballplayer was now following them . . .

The frog and swine Frankensteins went up two floors. Here, the stairs and corridors were almost deserted. Piggy pulled Kermit into a private box, leaving the door open a crack and peering out. She said in a low voice, "Maybe he's given up. Nope! Here he's coming down again!"

She tried to close the door, but Kermit prevented her; for he had seen, on the top step of the staircase that led to the floor above, one cleat descend into view, followed by another . . . and slowly the whole uniform met his eyes. He exclaimed, "It's the blue-skinned evil-genius hurdy-gurdy player of the churchyard at Cannes!"

She glanced back at him. "It's actually pronounced 'can.'"

"Piggy, that is none other than your Koozebanian of Music! I'm going to march out there, snatch off that helmet, stare him in the face, and . . . politely ask him to state his business!"

But with a tragic gesture, she closed the door and flung out her arms to block him. "Kermit, you cannot pass," she hissed. "Let him go back to the shadow. The dark fire is not to be trifled with! *You shall not PASS!*"

Was she just trying to gain a few seconds to give that blasted ballplayer time to escape? Unable to control himself, Kermit blurted, "I don't even know if you're telling the truth! What a patsy I must be to let you mock me like this! I didn't know that women were so eager to make fools of us men."

"Uh, I hate to break it to ya, but most of you are actually DIY types."

"I'm a pretty upbeat guy. I tend to look on the bright side. I mean, it helps that I literally eat what bugs me. But you're pushing me too far—and it's not just *me*! You've even taken advantage of *Mildred*, who believes your tall tales about lessons with an alien, while you run around the Opera with your, with your . . ." He gestured helplessly toward the door. "With your *tight end*!"

Piggy allowed him to say whatever he had to, with only one goal in mind: to keep him from going into the hallway and getting tackled. "*Vous* will be sorry one day for all those ugly words about *moi*, Kermit, and when you are, I will forgive you! But for now, adieu! You shall not see me again!"

"But you're free—you ran around Paris all these weeks, you put on a costume to come to a ball, you go to

Disneyland! Why don't you just go home? What is this hooey about the Koozebanian of Music that you've been telling Mildred? What is this farce?"

Piggy stepped closer to him and into the light, giving him his first clear glimpse of her face. She said, "Dear Kermie, this farce . . . is a *tragedy*!" Kermit now saw that hard, sad shadows covered those features that he had known to be so gentle and cheerful. "It is something that even five facials can't fix. I know because I had all five of them this morning!"

Resigned, she opened the door and stepped outside, forbidding him to follow with the threat of a karate chop.

He watched till she was out of sight. Then he went down among the crowd and spotted Pepé, who was wearing a sandwich board in the shape of a martini glass.

Kermit glanced at the costume. "What are you supposed to be?"

"A shrimp cocktail, okay. Ees joke. Funny, no?"

Kermit asked him if he had seen the helmeted menace. The prawn shook his head and added, "Anyway I think football ees overrated. They say ees supposed to build joor muscles, *sí*? I think that claim ees *loco*, because I watch *four* games last weekend, and I'm still super scrawny."

Although he kept searching, Kermit couldn't locate

his rival again. At two o'clock in the morning, as the supermodels were pleading for selfies with the STEM gang, Kermit found himself heading down the backstage passage that led to Piggy Daaé's dressing room, where he had first heard that strange voice.

He tapped at the door, but there was no answer. He entered and found it unoccupied. He heard footsteps approaching, so he ducked into the inner dressing area, which was separated from the main room by a curtain.

Piggy swept in, took off her wig with a weary movement, and flung it onto the table. She sighed and let her blond tresses cascade onto her sturdy shoulders. What was she thinking of? Of Kermit? Apparently not, as Kermit heard her murmur, "Poor Deadly!"

Wait—*what?* If anyone was to be pitied, it was *Kermit*. It would have been quite natural if she had said "Poor Kermit" after what had happened between them. But, shaking her head, she repeated, "Poor Uncle Deadly!"

Uncle? She had never mentioned having an uncle. As far as Kermit knew, neither Rowlf nor his wife had siblings. Who was this "Uncle Deadly," and what did he have to do with Piggy's sighs?

Suddenly she raised her head and listened. Kermit heard it, too: a faint something within the walls . . . Yes, it was as though the stones themselves were singing! The song became plainer, and the words more distinguishable. He heard a voice, a very beautiful, captivating male voice, accompanied by the peculiar whine of what he now knew was the hurdy-gurdy. It sang about desert highways, cool wind in the hair . . . It sounded far away in the distance, beyond the room's shimmering lights. Kermit had to grab the handle—his head grew heavy and his sight grew dim. (There was a mop to his right.)

When he looked up again, there she stood in the doorway. He saw her resolve swell. She muttered to herself, "This could be heaven or this could be hell."

The voice was now *in the room*, in front of Piggy, who addressed it: "Okay, Uncle Deadly," she said. "It's go time!"

Kermit, peeping from behind the curtain, couldn't believe his eyes. Besides Piggy, there was no one there! The voice without a body went on singing, and certainly Kermit had never in his life heard anything more absolutely and heroically sweet, more gloriously insidious or more powerful, at least since *NSYNC broke up.

Hearing this voice now, he began to understand how Piggy was able to appear before the stupefied audience, crooning with a beauty hitherto unknown, clearly under the influence of her mysterious and invisible instructor.

Kermit saw Piggy stretch out her arms to the voice,

as she had done in the graveyard to the invisible hurdy-gurdy, and nothing could describe the passion with which this voice again sang.

Struggling against the charm that seemed to deprive him of all his will and all his energy and of almost all his sanity at the moment when he needed them most, Kermit drew back the curtain that hid him and walked to Piggy, intending to confront her. She was moving toward the back of the room, the whole wall of which was occupied by a great mirror that reflected her image— but not *his* image, for he was just behind her, and she entirely covered him from her view.

She walked toward herself in the glass, and her image came toward her. The hypnotic singing reached a crescendo as the two Piggys—the physical one and the reflection—stopped, nearly touching. Kermit reached out to embrace the two, but, by a sort of dazzling miracle that sent him staggering, he was suddenly flung back by an icy blast. He saw not two, but four, eight, twenty Piggys spinning around him, disappearing so swiftly that he could not touch any of them.

At last, everything stood still again, and he saw only himself in the glass.

Piggy was gone!

He rushed to the mirror and struck at the glass.

Nobody! Which way had Piggy gone? Which way would she return? *Would* she return? Alas, had she not declared to him that everything was finished? And meanwhile the room still echoed with a distant passionate singing:

> *"'Relax,' said the night man, 'we are programmed to receive,*
> *You can check out any time you like,*
> *but you can never leave!'"*

Leave *what*? Leave *where*?

Worn-out, beaten, and empty-brained, he sat down on the chair and let his head fall into his hands.

When he finally looked up again, tears were streaming down his green cheeks—real, heavy tears like those shed by jealous children and rejected *Bachelor* contestants, tears that wept for a sorrow that was in no way fanciful, but which is common to all the lovers on earth and which he expressed aloud, shaking a defiant frog fist: *"I will find this Uncle Deadly!"*

Chapter X
IXNAY ON THE OOZEBANIANKAY

The day after Piggy had vanished before his eyes in a sort of dazzlement that still made him wonder whether he should have his head examined, Monsieur le Vicomte Kermit de Chagny visited Mildred Huxtetter's apartment.

What he found there was bewildering: Piggy herself was seated by the bedside of the old lady, who was propped up against the pillows, knitting. The pink had returned to Piggy's cheeks, and the dark circles around her eyes had disappeared. She was happily snacking on Funyuns and sending a pack of cats scrambling to and fro in blissful delirium with a laser pointer.

When she saw him, Piggy stood without showing any emotion and offered him her hand. But Kermit's stupefaction was so great that he just waited there dumbfounded.

"Well, Monsieur de Chagny," exclaimed Mildred,

"don't you know our Piggy? Her good Koozebanian has sent her back to us!"

"Mother Mildred!" the pig broke in promptly, blushing deeply. "Ixnay on the Oozebaniankay! Remember? There is no such thing!"

"But, child, he must exist. He taught you lessons for three months. He persuaded the managers to let you play Siebel. And he's got a verified Twitter account!"

"Look, I've promised to explain everything to you one of these days," Piggy grumbled, "but you have promised me, until then, to stop asking me questions!"

"Provided that you promised never to leave me again. But have you promised that, Piggy?"

"*Seriously*—all this claptrap cannot interest Kermit."

"I love claptrap!" said the frog in a voice that he tried to make firm and brave but which still trembled. "I'm most definitely interested in anything that concerns you. I just wish you'd stop all this secrecy—it's dangerous, and we've been friends for too long for me to not be alarmed, like Mildred, by what seems like some really wacky behavior."

Piggy gave him the stink eye.

"Dangerous?" cried Mildred Huxtetter, involuntarily squeezing a nearby cat's tail. The freaked-out feline yowled. "What do you mean?" she cried, sitting up. "Is Piggy in danger?"

"I think she might be," said Kermit, ignoring Piggy's urgent gesticulating behind Mildred's back. "Some impostor is taking advantage of her talent, which definitely isn't charades."

Mildred pressed further: "Is the Koozebanian of Music an impostor?"

"Ixnay on the Oozebaniankay, I said!" growled Piggy.

"But then what is it?"

Kermit stepped closer to the old woman. "There is a terrible mystery around Piggy, Madame, a mystery much scarier than any ghost, or goblin, or vampire, or that other thing, the one with the bandages—"

"Mummy! Don't believe him," Piggy pleaded with Mildred.

"Then tell me that you will never leave me again," urged the widow.

Piggy was silent, so Kermit resumed. "Sounds fair, Piggy, and it's a good way to reassure us. Let's make a deal: We won't ask you a single question about the past if you promise to let us protect you in the future."

"Listen up, buster. I never asked for your protection, and I'm not about to make any promises to you," she retorted haughtily.

"Well, that was a haughty retort," he noted.

"This is *my* business. I'm the boss of me. Heck, I don't

just lean in, I *fall over*. There's only one man in the world who has the right to ask me those kinds of questions— besides the guy that's ghostwriting my autobiography— and that's my husband! Well, I don't have a husband, and I'm never getting married!"

She threw out her hands to emphasize her words, and Kermit turned pale, not only because of what she'd said, but because of what he saw: a *ring* on Piggy's finger! A ruby of enormous proportions!

He stammered, "Y-y-you don't have a husband, but you're wearing a ring . . ." Then he got a better look at it. ". . . *pop*. You're wearing a lollipop ring?"

He tried to seize her hand, but she swiftly drew it back. "It's nothing!"

"If it's nothing, why haven't you eaten it?"

"I'm on a diet."

"Balderdash!" said Kermit.

"It's the all-garlic-all-day diet. You don't lose weight, but from a distance everyone thinks you look thinner."

"Phooey! That ring is a promise—and one that's clearly been accepted!"

"That's what *I* said!" exclaimed the old lady.

"Mummy, put a lid on it, will ya!" Piggy was driven to exasperation. She paused and took a deep breath. "Don't you think, monsieur, that you've put me through enough grilling? I'm not a T-bone!"

Kermit held up his hands in surrender. "Okay, okay, I'm sorry, it's just that I really don't want you to get hurt. And from what I've seen . . ."

"Yes, why don't you tell us what you saw—or *thought* you saw," challenged Piggy.

"I saw you under a dangerous spell at the sound of the voice, Piggy, that voice singing its classic California rock from inside the walls. And it seems like you're trying to cover it all up, saying today *that there is no Koozebanian of Music*! If that's true, why did you stand there hypnotized as though you were really hearing voices from somewhere out in the galaxy? Tell us who's behind that voice, Piggy. Tell us who put that precious Ring Pop on your finger. Tell us that your Koozebanian is actually named Uncle Deadly!"

Piggy was flabbergasted. "Who told you his name?"

"You did! The night of the ball. When you went to your dressing room, you said, 'Poor Uncle Deadly'! Well, Piggy, there was a 'poor Kermit' who overheard you."

"What is it with you and snooping! And are you determined to get hurt? Don't you know that Deadly is a *squisher*?! Promise me you'll drop all this. Promise me you won't surprise me in my dressing room unless I send for you."

"So you will send for me sometimes, Piggy?"

"Yes, I will. Cross my heart and hope to—"

Kermit blurted, "Ixnay!"

Before parting, he kissed her hand—not the one with the rascal's Ring Pop, but the other—and he thought, *Ah, Funyuns . . . I'll cherish that heavenly fragrance forever . . .*

Chapter XI
OTHERWISE ENGAGED

To Kermit's surprise, Piggy invited him to visit her at the Opera the very next day. She was still wearing the Ring Pop, but he barely noticed, preoccupied with some troubling news he'd received that morning.

After some friendly chitchat, he broke it to her that the date of his North Pole expedition, the final part of his naval training, had been moved forward.

"What are you saying?" she asked, confused.

He explained that he would now be leaving France sooner, in three weeks or a month at the latest. "So . . . ," he continued, bowing his head, his pulse racing. "I guess I'm just a frog, standing in front of a pig, asking her to love him." He swallowed hard. "What if . . . until I leave . . ." *Oh boy*, he thought, *am I really going to do this?* "What if we decided to maybe get engaged—"

"Impossible!" But she seemed suddenly almost unable to contain an overpowering happiness, clapping her hands with childish glee. "Then again, my Kermie-wermie," she continued, holding out her hands to the frog, or rather giving them to him, as though she had suddenly resolved to make him a present of them, "we could *pretend* to be engaged! Nobody has to know but us. There have been plenty of secret weddings—just off the top of my head, Brad Pitt and Jennifer Aniston, Chris Martin and Gwyneth Paltrow, Ryan Reynolds and Scarlett Johansson—"

"Um, none of those marriages lasted—"

"My point *is*, we could have a secret *engagement*! One month of bliss, then au revoir, off you go!"

Kermit jumped at the idea. Literally. He couldn't control his excitement, and he leaped into the air.

"Oh, Kermie, how happy we will be! We must play at being engaged all day long."

And they did so all that day.

Then they did it again the next day, and continued for a whole week more.

They obsessively played at being engaged, as geeks might play Pokémon Go—until Kermit, unable to think of parting after the bliss of these seven days, uttered thirty-three wild, life-altering words: "I've changed my mind: I'm *not* going to go to the North Pole, after all! I mean, obviously Santa is an *amazing* hider or they would have found him by now! It's pointless!"

And suddenly everything changed.

Piggy looked at him like he was off his rocker. She hadn't dreamed he would stay in Paris, and she realized that this game of pretend was too dangerous to continue. She dashed to the curb and, with a shrill whistle, hailed a carriage and went straight home. That evening, she called in sick.

The next morning, a distraught Kermit hurried to see Mildred Huxtetter. While pruning a pot of catnip, she told him that Piggy had left the afternoon before and said she would be away for two days.

True to her word, Piggy returned on the following night. And she returned in triumph onstage. Since the performance of the scene-stealing "cow," Yolanda had been an utter wreck. Mama Fiama told the players at the Opera that Dr. Honeydew had diagnosed it as acute stage fright, "but the symptoms, what they do to her is not a-cute at all," she added. "He say Yolanda's whiskers, they have fallen out from-a the stress!"

The terror of a fresh "moo" deprived the rat of any confidence in her singing. She had locked herself away in her town house, where she spent her days Internet-trolling Piggy. Because, to add insult to perceived injury, Statler and Waldorf had suddenly promoted Piggy to

Yolanda's spot in the company!

The next day Kermit found Piggy in her dressing room, cheerfully munching on Cheetos. She suggested they take a walk, but instead of strolling outside, she took him to the stage and they wandered along the deserted paths of a garden whose blooms had been cut out by a decorator's skillful hands. Later, she dragged him up above the painted clouds to the magnificent disorder of the grid, where she unknowingly incited panic by tromping along the frail suspended bridges, sending the terrified penguins below scurrying for shelter.

Then they returned to terra firma, that is to say, to some passage that led them to the little chicks' dancing school, where Piggy gave gummy worms to the young birds who were practicing their steps in hopes of one day becoming the next Janice Sorelli. "Remember, darlings: You're all one of a kind," Piggy told them sagely. "And that kind is 'marginally talented.'"

She took Kermit on an exhaustive tour of the wardrobe and property rooms and to all the areas of her immense empire, which was inhabited by an army of costumers, cobblers, painters, ironworkers, and more. She moved among them like a queen, encouraging them and doling out words of wisdom. "Always find something to complain about, no matter how small or insignificant," she advised. "Everyone will respect your professional attention to detail."

At one point, when they were passing an open trapdoor on the stage, Kermit peered below into the darkness. "You've shown me all over the upper part of the Opera, Piggy, but I've heard some very strange stories about the lower part. Should we go down?"

"Never! You can't go down there!" She body-blocked him, then took a moment to regain her composure. "Everything that is underground belongs to . . . him."

Kermit raised an eyebrow. "So he lives down there, does he?"

"Come along! Let's go!" And as she dragged him away, the trap shut with a sudden *slam*—so quickly, they didn't even see the hand that did it.

"Okay, that was creepy," Kermit whispered.

She shrugged, but her pretend indifference was betrayed by the shaking Ring Pop on her trembling hand. "He's composing. He can't open and shut the trapdoors and work at the same time." A shiver passed through her. "But it's all the better for us. When he's working, he pays no attention to me. I know, hard to imagine."

Her agitation only increased as she dragged the now-exhausted frog up to the topmost floor of the theater, far from the trapdoors. But that still wasn't far enough away for her. "Higher!" she cried. "Higher still!"

Despite how often she looked behind them, she failed to notice a shadow that followed the pair like their own shadows, which stopped when they stopped, which started again when they did, and which made no more noise than a well-conducted shadow should.

Chapter XII

AND THE STORM BEGINS TO FORM

The shadow had tiptoed behind them, clinging to their steps, and the giddy pair little suspected its presence when they finally emerged onto the roof.

There, they saw that Janice Sorelli had rolled out her mat in a far corner and was doing yoga in the final throes of the spring sunlight. "OMG, hi," Janice called to them in upside-down greeting. "You guys wanna join? This headstand, like, totally flushes out your adrenal glands."

"Ick, sounds messy," replied Piggy.

Kermit shook his head. "I tried yoga once, but I found it a bit of a stretch."

Piggy took Kermit's hand. "We're just going to sit over there and watch the sunset."

"Groovy," said Janice, "because honestly, Piggy, you've been looking rilly pale lately. I'm glad you're getting some fresh air and vitamin D. You know what they say: A day without sunshine is, like, night."

The couple strolled past the great gilded cupola of the auditorium and admired the statues along the roof's edge, great marble likenesses of iconic music figures and the instruments that had made them famous: Apollo and his lyre, Pan and his flute, Ariana Grande and her ponytail.

They sat down out of earshot under the mighty protection of Elvis Presley, who, with a grand gesture, lifted his huge guitar up to the gold, crimson, and purple sunset sky.[25]

Clouds drifted slowly by. Kermit and Piggy named the shapes they saw in the fluffy stuff. He pointed out a parakeet, a top hat, and a sailboat, while she spied a hoagie, a chimichanga, and a tuna casserole.

Kermit was so happy to see Piggy out of doors, breathing freely. She turned to him and confessed, "Oh, Kermie, I don't want to go back to live with him in the ground!"

"So don't go!"

"Well, thank you, Captain Duh. But if I don't go back to him, something *très* awful may happen!"

Kermit scooted closer. "Then let's leave right now.

---

[25] This stone Elvis figure, it may here be mentioned, was both ornamental and practical, for his six-string was tipped with a metal point that did double duty as a lightning rod. When a strike occurred and a bolt connected, the instrument literally became the world's first electric guitar.

I can take you away from him!"

"No, no," she said, shaking her head. "It would be too cruel to make him go cold turkey on this pig. I have to let him hear me sing tomorrow evening. I owe him that much after all the lessons he's given me. So tomorrow night, you must come and find me afterward in my dressing room at midnight exactly, and away we'll go."

She gave a sigh, and another sigh from somewhere behind them seemed to reply in kind. Kermit whispered, "Um, diiiiiiiid you hear that?"

They stood up and surveyed the roof. Janice was now sitting, eyes closed, in a deep silent meditation. Otherwise they seemed to be quite alone.

"Those yoga people make some strange sounds," said Piggy. "Oh, it really stinks to always be nervous like this! I know I shouldn't be. He can't hear me outside the walls of the Opera House, up here in the sky, in the open air."

They sat down again, and Kermit said, "Tell me how you first saw him."

"Well, I didn't actually lay eyes on him for a long time. For three months I had heard that mysterious voice when I was in my dressing room. And it didn't just sing— it actually spoke to me! It gave me stock tips, fashion advice, totally fabulous gossip. I told Mildred, and she said it had to be the Koozebanian of Music, the very voice that my father had promised me. When I asked the Voice if that was true, it immediately said yes. It went on to say, 'I'd like to give you lessons every day—for free! Would you like that?' And I was all, 'Does an armadillo like grubs? *Of course!*' After a few weeks of studying with him, my A game had become an A-plus game! I shocked even myself. I can humbly state that, as brilliant as I had been before, the lessons had made me *even more* brilliant. Now I was brilliant smothered in awesomesauce."

Kermit smiled.

"Then one night, there you were, in the audience, my childhood friend. Smiling just like that. I didn't even think to hide my delight when I got back to my dressing room. But when I told the Voice about you, it went all silent and pouty. That night, I went home feeling awful, even worse than that time I missed the spring sample sale at Marc Jacobs. Mildred explained it, saying, 'Why, of course, the Voice is jealous!'"

Piggy stopped and laid her head on his shoulder. "And that, dear Kermie, first made it obvious to me how *moi* felt about *toi*." They sat like that for a moment looking out over the towers of Notre-Dame and failed to notice, just a few steps away, the creeping shadow that came along the roof so near . . .

"The next day," Piggy continued, "the Voice was back

in my dressing room, *très* miffed, and said, 'If you are going to bestow your heart on Earth, there is nothing for me to do but to go back to Koozebane.' I was afraid that I might never hear it again, and I couldn't let my career go—how can I put this as delicately as possible—into the crapper. And besides, your position in society meant we could never be together . . . or so I thought." She batted her luxurious lashes at him. "For all those reasons, I swore to the Voice that you were no more than a pal to me. And that, Kermie, was why I avoided you all those times you came to the Opera, and why I became such a brat. Because, like Big Brother, the Voice is always listening!"

She looked around again suspiciously, then continued. "Meanwhile, we practiced together like crazy, until, at last, the Voice said to me, 'Now it's time to give Paris a little taste of the Koozebane.' I have no idea why Yolanda called in sick that night or why Grosse picked me to sing 'Mahna Mahna' in her place. But a girl's gotta make the most of her big break, so I sang my face off."

"And when you opened your eyes after fainting," recalled Kermit, "I was there."

"Yes you were, my Kermie. And Dr. Honeydew, too. But the Voice was there, as well! So I pretended I didn't know you and played dumb when you talked about going into the sea for my Jet Ski. But there's no tricking the

Voice. It figured out who you were, and it was jealous! Oh, the *drama* I got from that one! It said that if I did not love you, I would treat you like any other old friend. Finally, I was like, 'Enough already! I'm taking a trip to the beach at Cannes tomorrow to visit my father's grave, see some movies, and have a Nathan's Famous hot dog.' The Voice said, 'Do as you please, but I'll be there, too. Like carbohydrate cravings, I am wherever you are. And, if you are still worthy of my attention, if you have not fibbed to me about loving that amphibian, be in the graveyard at the stroke of midnight, and I will wow you with 'Stairway to Heaven' on the hurdy-gurdy.'"

"Huh. Such a strange instrument," mused Kermit. "Do you like its sound?"

"It's not bad, but I'm really all about that bass."

There was a long silence between the three of them: the two who spoke and the shadow that listened behind them . . .

"Oh, Kermit, how did I not figure out that he was a faker? I've seen *every* episode of *Catfish*!"

"But then when you *did* figure it out," Kermit replied, "why didn't you run away?"

"By the time I learned the truth, it was too late. You remember that evening when Yolanda thought she had been turned into a cow onstage, and when the chandelier

156

brutally killed Beaker, and blah blah blah? Well, once I was back in my dressing room, I heard a new song coming through the walls, and I was drawn to it. It was like the first time I ate Sour Patch Kids: I just lost control of my senses. I stood up and started walking toward the mirrored wall of my dressing room, and—this was the craziest thing!—as I moved, my dressing room seemed to lengthen out . . . then, suddenly, I was outside the room without knowing how!"

"Where were you?"

"In a dim, creepy secret passage. It was dead silent, then I saw a cloaked shape wearing one of those *lucha libre* Mexican wrestling masks with bedazzled bits. I was about to karate chop him when I realized there was another, much larger shape nearby. I could just make out the two humps on its back. Then it spit a big loogie, and a sweeter sound I never heard. It was Sopwith, the brown camel that I had so often shared my Cracker Jacks with. And then the masked shape started singing again, and I must have fallen under his spell, because the next thing I knew I was sitting between those two humps on the camel's back, trudging through the darkness behind the cloaked shape."

"I remember hearing a rumor backstage that the camel had disappeared from the stables," said Kermit, "and some thought it must have been stolen by the Phantom."

Piggy nodded. "Bingo! That was when I finally put it all together: I believed in the Voice, but I'd never believed in the Phantom. Now I began to wonder if the Voice and the Phantom *were one and the same*! As I was thinking this, we were moving along a narrow circular underground passageway. Sopwith kept walking and walking, turning and turning, and spitting and spitting, into what seemed like the very heart of the Earth. Those cellars are gigantic—I'm talking *Costco-size*. Eventually we reached an underground lake, and the cloaked creature helped me into a little swan-shaped paddleboat. As fast as he peddled, the boat still barely inched along. It took *forever* for him to ferry us all the way across, but those green eyes, glowing under the mask, never left me. When we reached the opposite shore, we descended a staircase to another massive cellar below, and I found myself on an actual carnival midway, with blinking lights, game booths, rides, and all! And the black shape of the thing in the mask finally said, 'Don't be afraid, Piggy.' And *bam*, that was when I knew: *It was the Voice!*"

Kermit's eyes were wide. "What did you do?"

"I rushed at the mask and tried to snatch it away, but he backed up and said, 'You are in no danger—so long as you keep your mitts off the mask, missy.' I looked around the midway of this bizarre, eccentric person who had somehow created a carnival five stories beneath an opera house. And the Voice confessed, 'It is true! I am not a Koozebanian, nor a genius, nor a ghost . . .'"

Piggy paused in her telling, and a dramatic rumble of thunder punctuated the moment like a drumroll.

"'Don't be angry with me, dear Piggy,' he said, 'but I am none of those things . . .'"

Pops of lightning inside a looming cloud above them strobed on their faces as she finished her sentence. "Finally, he confessed: 'The fact of the matter is, I am just plain *Uncle Deadly*!'"

An echo behind Piggy and Kermit seemed to repeat the word after her: *"Deadly!"* They both suddenly became aware that night had fallen. Janice was long gone. And even though they thought they'd heard a voice, they could see no one else on the roof.

"Well, now that we know that Uncle Deadly is no ghost," said Kermit, "I can go into the cellars and search—"

"No! There is nothing to be done with Deadly . . . except to run away! He is seriously fifty shades of cray. You should have seen his home: It's inside a fun house. There are shifting and wobbly floors, an entire room tilted at forty-five degrees, surprise blasts of freezing cold air—it's like a New York City apartment, but *on purpose*."

Kermit asked, "How long did he make you stay?"

"'You will be free, Piggy,' he told me, 'when five days are past, because you will have learned not to be afraid of me. And then, from time to time, you will come to visit your poor Deadly!' Then he took me to his midway, where we rode the Tilt-A-Whirl, the free fall, and the Zipper. After that, I ate a balanced meal of deep-fried grilled cheese, deep-fried pizza, deep-fried Oreos, and deep-fried cotton candy."

"Um," he interrupted, "how exactly are those four things *balanced*?"

"Easy: two in each hand."

She tucked a lock of hair behind her ear and continued. "He also showed me his mask room. It was like a Halloween costume shop. The entire wall was covered in masks of all kinds: clown masks, feathered Mardi Gras masks, ski masks, gas masks, Jim Carrey's *The Mask* mask. On the desk I noticed sheets of music, their staves dotted with red-inked notes. I got a peek at the title: 'The Storm Cloud Connection.' He told me he'd been composing the piece for twenty years and that it was the work of his life. I asked him to play me some of it, thinking it would flatter him. But he shook his head and said, 'Only when it's finished.' It was then that I finally felt fear, a deep terror that arose with a certain dawning revelation." She trailed off, as if the words were too terrible to utter.

Kermit gently tried to draw her out. "What was this terrible discovery?"

"I realized that I'd seen *no mirrors in the whole carnival.*" She shuddered. "Who could live like that?! Suddenly I felt a need to see beneath the mask, and, just like that, I tore it away. Oh, horror, horror, horror!"

The echoes of the night, which had repeated the name of Deadly, now thrice echoed the cry: "Horrorrrr . . . Horrorrrr . . . Horrorrrr . . ."

Kermit and Piggy, clasping each other closely, raised their eyes to the few stars that managed to peek through the rapidly crowding cloudscape. He whispered, "It's strange, Piggy, that this night should be so full of sad sounds."

She took Kermit's protecting hands in hers and, with a long shiver, continued. "Oh, the cry of grief and rage that Deadly uttered! Oh, the face—imagine, if you can, a blue dragon as furious as a demon, green eyes piercing, *and not a ray of light from its eye sockets.* Leaning over me, he shouted, 'You want to see? Look at Deadly's face! Now that you know the face of the Voice, you can never leave me again!' And then he turned to his hurdy-gurdy and started jamming. And I gotta admit, his 'Storm Cloud Connection' was pretty dope. It was the kind of song I'd totally Spotify *on repeat*. I started to feel bad. 'Deadly,' I said, 'turn around and show me your face without shame! I'm cool with it, I swear. If I ever again shiver when I look at you, it will only be because I'm thinking of how genius this track is!' Then Deadly stopped playing and turned, because I'm an astonishing actress and he believed me, even though I secretly still found him pretty ghoulish. But he put the mask back on, anyway."

Her eyes searched Kermit's face. "So what more can I tell you, *mon petit chou*? You now know the whole shebang. It went on for nearly two weeks—two weeks during which I fibbed that I wasn't afraid, but those fibs were the price of my liberty. I lived in his fun house, and gradually I gave him such confidence that he took me to play skee ball and ringtoss, and he paddled me around the lake in that ridiculously poky swan boat. Then, at last, after two weeks of carny life underground, during which I was filled with despair and horror—"

"Because of his looks?"

"No, because of *mine*—I had to do my hair in the reflection of a serving spoon! *Finally*, he believed me when I told him I would come back."

"And you did," groaned Kermit.

"*Oui.* Because I felt sorry for the guy. Not everyone has my devastating looks and bulletproof self-esteem. Let's face it: I put the *I* in *moi.* But now . . . He's getting odder. Instead of calming him, each of my visits seems to make him more mad with love!"

"But, Piggy? I have to ask: If Deadly was a hottie, would you still care for me?"

She stood up and put her arms around the young frog's neck. "Oh, my pretend fiancé of a week, you're all that and a bag of chips. And you know how I feel about chips!"

But before they could get to any mushy stuff, the dark night sky was suddenly lit by a mammoth crack of lightning. Had they not fled from the storm's violent cloudburst, they might have been all shook up to see a pair of bulging eyes peering at them from behind Elvis's marble pelvis . . .

Chapter XIII

DROP IN AND SEE ME SOMETIME

Kermit and Piggy skedaddled, and they didn't pause on the way down until they hit the eighth floor. There was no performance at the Opera that night, and the passages were empty. Suddenly an odd-looking form blocked their path: "No, not this way!" It pointed a furry finger to another passage: "Quick, go that way!"

Kermit wanted ask who that was, but before he could catch his breath, Piggy dragged him along. Finally, they dashed into the star's dressing room on the second floor.

Kermit looked around. "Is *he* listening?"

She held a finger to her lips and whispered her reply. "Deadly can hear me anywhere inside the Opera House."

Kermit said in a low voice, "Are you still determined to run away from him?"

"Absoposilutely."

"Then I'll be here at twelve tomorrow night. You can count on it."

Just then Piggy gasped. A mortal pallor spread across her features as she stared at her hand. "The Ring Pop! The candy ring he gave me!"

"So Deadly *did* give you that ring!"

"Oh, puh-*leaze*, Kermit! You know he did. But what you don't know is that when he slipped it on my finger, he said, 'I give you back your freedom on the condition that you always wear this. As long as you keep it, you will be protected against all danger, and Deadly will remain your friend. But woe to you if you ever part with it, for Deadly will have his revenge!'"

Kermit shook his head, impressed. "You have remarkable recall for dialogue."

"Now the ring is *gone*! Darn this early prototype plastic! Woe is totally me!"

She dashed out, wringing and rubbing her fingers, as though she hoped to bring the ring back like that.

Completely flipping out at all that he had heard, Kermit made his way home. Constantine had returned from his date with Janice and was already fast asleep. So Kermit fed Foo-Foo, said good night to Angus, and hit the hay.

"If I don't save her from the hands of that no-goodnik, she will be lost," he said aloud to himself as he got into bed, put out his lamp, and pulled his teddy bear close. "But with Mr. Snuggles as my witness, I *will* save her." He felt a need to curse Uncle Deadly in the dark. Thrice over, he grumbled: "Humbug! Humbug! Humbug!" (He was not a very good curser.)

Suddenly he raised himself up on his elbow as cold sweat formed on his temples: Two green eyes, like blazing peas, had appeared at the foot of his bed! They stared at him in the darkness of the night.

Kermit was no coward, but he couldn't help but tremble. He reached a hesitating hand toward his bedside table, found the matches, and lit a candle. The eyes disappeared.

Still uneasy, he said to himself, "*Deadly's* eyes only show in the dark . . ." He rose and hunted about. He looked under his bed like a child, and saw a monstrous . . . dust bunny. Angus was clearly shirking his duties.

He thought himself absurd, got into bed again, and blew out the candle.

The eyes reappeared! *What the what?!*

He sat up and stared back at them with all the courage he possessed. Then he realized: *He's on the balcony!*

Kermit went to the balcony door cautiously and opened it. Seeing nothing, he closed the door again, went to the chest of drawers, and grabbed his slingshot and a few marbles. He got back in bed, shivering, for the night was cold, and set the slingshot on the table within reach.

He dared to look again: The eyes were still there, at the foot of the bed! Patiently, calmly, he seized his slingshot and aimed a little above the two eyes. Surely, if they were eyes, and if above those two eyes there was a forehead, and if Kermit was not too clumsy . . .

The marble smashed right through the glass and made a terrible din amid the silence of the slumbering house. Foo-Foo's barks echoed as footsteps came hurrying along the passages. Kermit sat up with an outstretched arm, ready to pop off another, if need be.

"Crivens!" said Angus MacGregor as he stepped into the room carrying a lantern.

Count Constantine arrived next, rubbing his sleepy eyes, and said, "Vat eez goingk on?"

"I think I've been dreaming," replied the young frog. "Two stars kept me from sleeping, so I tried to put them out."

"Vat eez dis ravingk! You are ill? Vat has happened, brother ov mine?"

"We will soon see . . ." Kermit got out of bed and put on his slippers. He took the light from Angus and, opening the door, stepped out onto the balcony, glass crunching underfoot. "Aha!" he said, pointing. "Blood!

Here, there, more blood! That's a good thing! A ghost who bleeds is less dangerous!" He grinned madly.

"Kermit!" The count was shaking him like a maraca. "You are sleepvalkingk? You have gone mad I am thinkingk!"

From outside, Angus called to Constantine. "Mehbe noot, Count; aye, there be blood on the balconeh."

They examined it carefully and found that the red drops followed the rail till they reached a gutter spout. Then they appeared to go up the gutter spout.

"Brother," said Constantine, "I think you haf pegged a pigeon."

"Well, it is quite possible," said Kermit, with a crooked smile. "Is it a ghost? Is it a pigeon? Is it a blue lizard-dragon named Uncle Deadly? Who can tell?"

"Who eez dis 'Deadly'?" asked the count.

"He's my rival. And if I missed him with my marble, it's a pity."

Constantine sent Angus back to bed, and the two Chagnys were left alone. But the butler was not out of earshot before he heard Kermit say, distinctly and emphatically: "I plan to run away with Piggy tomorrow night." Angus reported this phrase afterward to Fozzie Bear. But no one ever knew exactly what else passed between the two brothers.

At breakfast the next morning, Kermit arrived silent and gloomy. Constantine handed him a Pop-Tart and a copy of Fleet Scribbler's gossip column, the Daily Scandale. The viscount read:

"The latest news in the Faubourg is that Mlle. Piggy Daaé, the opera singer, and M. le Vicomte Kermit de Chagny are getting hitched! If the Internet has it right (and doesn't it always?), Count Constantine has sworn that, for the first time on record, the Chagnys shall not keep their promise. But as love is all-powerful, especially at the Opera, we wonder how Count Constantine intends to stop Kermit from leading his salty Margarita to the altar. The siblings are said to adore each other, but the count is curiously mistaken if he imagines that brotherly love will triumph over love pure and simple. Only in Paris, kids, only in Paris."

"Ridiculous eez how you are maikink us look!" exclaimed the count. "Leetle pig has scrambled your head talkink of ghosts. You haf made up your mind? You are goingk tonight? With her?"

No reply.

"Try to do anythingk dangerous, Kermit, and I *am* goingk to stop you!"

"So long, Constantine," said the viscount, and he left.

This scene was described to Fozzie Bear by the count himself, who did not see Kermit again until that evening, at the Opera, a few minutes before Piggy's disappearance, a startling event about which you will soon hear.

But that day, Kermit devoted every minute to his secret preparations for the escape. He Google Map'd the route and withdrew cash from the ATM. He arranged the carriage, the coachman, the pretzels.

He didn't finish till nine o'clock at night, when a certain carriage took its place on a side street bordering the Opera House. It was driven by a coachman whose face was almost fully concealed in the long folds of a muffler but whose telltale claw was un-mittened. In front of this carriage were three others: at the head of the line, one for Comte Constantine de Chagny; behind that, one for Yolanda (you can't keep a devious diva down for long); and last, one for Janice Sorelli (hers was a hybrid, naturally).

A shadow in a long black cloak and a black ski mask that covered its entire head stole along the pavement between the Opera House and the carriages, examining them all carefully, then moved away without saying a word.

Afterward, Fozzie believed that this masked figure must have been the Vicomte Kermit de Chagny. But I don't agree. I am more inclined to think that the shadow was that of the Phantom, who somehow already knew all about the whole affair, as the reader will soon perceive.

Outside the Opera House's front doors, scalpers were trying to unload tickets for the night's performance. "What the heck is *Faust*?" asked a potential buyer. "I came to see *Hamilton*."

"Wrong theater," the scalper informed him. "That's playing three blocks over and two centuries away."

Backstage, Pepé was prepping the performers, giving them their half-hour call. "It's time to put on makeup, okay, it's time to light the lights. It's time to get the things started!"

Faust was attended that evening by an especially attentive audience. The gossips were out in full force. Fleet Scribbler's column in that morning's paper had already produced its effect: All eyes were turned to the box in which Count Constantine sat alone, feigning indifference and eating Twizzlers (he was partial to anything red).

And where, wondered the gossips, was the viscount?

Statler and Waldorf were schmoozing their most notable donors in the foyer, enduring the required glad-handing and small talk until, finally, they backed out of the room, bowing politely to all the bigwigs.

The first act went off without a hitch, and after a seemingly unremarkable intermission, act 2 began. Piggy Daaé made her entrance, and for the first time in recent memory, she was met with a rather cold reception. The catty members of the audience could not forgive her for aiming so high in her romantic aspirations.

Piggy's self-assurance drained. She trembled. She thought she might be on the verge of a breakdown. People recalled the catastrophe that had befallen Yolanda and the historic "moo" that had derailed her career. Could Piggy herself be headed for such a disaster?

Speak of the devil: Just then Yolanda swept into the auditorium, timing her entrance perfectly to create the biggest disruption. She confidently smoothed down her whiskers, which were just beginning to grow back. Piggy thought she saw a sneer from the snooty soprano as she stepped into her box and settled into the booster seat Mama Fiama had provided.

That sneer saved Piggy. "If you think you can psych out this superior specimen, you better think again," she muttered under her breath. "Because it's not over till the phat lady sings!"

The proud pig then warbled with all her heart and soul. She tried to top all that she had done till then—and she succeeded. In the center of the audience, a rapt patron stood up and remained standing, facing the singer. It was him! It was her Kermie-wermie!

And Piggy—her throat filled with music, her stomach filled with Hot Pockets—hit a glorious high note with her arms outstretched just as Johnny Fiama's Faust was making his cross to embrace her. At that moment *the stage was suddenly plunged into darkness*. It happened so quickly that the spectators hardly had time to gasp before the lights at once blazed again.

Johnny stood in the same spot, hugging himself. Because—astonishment!—Piggy Daaé was gone!

What had become of her? All exchanged glances without understanding, and the excitement surged. The penguins rushed from the wings to the spot where Piggy had been singing only an instant ago. Janice, the entire chorus, and the *corps de poulet* stood staring, mouths and beaks agape. *Where had Piggy gone?*

Still standing at his seat in the amphitheater, Kermit uttered a distressed *ribbit*. In his box, Count Constantine sprang to his feet. People looked at the stage, at the count, at Kermit, and wondered if this curious event was connected in any way with Fleet Scribbler's scribblings. But Kermit rushed out, and the count quickly followed suit.

After a few chaotic moments, Johnny Fiama and

Janice Sorelli stepped to the lip of the stage. In the musicians' pit, Lew Zealand ducked down, clutching his fish, perhaps fearing that it, too, might go missing.

In a sad and serious voice, Janice said, "Um, ladies and gents, something, like, totally trippy just went down. Piggy has disappeared before our eyes and we are fuh-*reak*ing out."

"And lemme just say," Johnny cut in, suddenly sentimental, "if any'a yous put a hit on that pig, I will find out and I will fight ya. You do *not* want to cross a Fiama!"

In the back of the theater, unseen, a small, suspicious smile spread across the ancient face of Mama Fiama. She told herself, "What my boy don't-a know won't-a hurt him . . ."

Chapter XIV

ONE ABSOLUTELY KRAZY NIGHT

An immediate examination by the diligent penguins of the trapdoors and stage floorboards soon put the idea of an accident out of the question.[26] Nevertheless, behind the curtain, the stage and its wings remained a full-on free-for-all. Performers, sceneshifters, dancers, and subscribers were all shouting and jostling one another, wondering what had become of her.

"She's run away."

"With the Vicomte Kermit, of course!"

"No, with Comte Constantine, I bet!"

"Unless it was *the Phantom!*"

Amid this noisy throng, three figures stood urgently talking in low voices. They were the business manager, Sam Eagle; Rizzo, the secretary; and Scooter, the assistant

---

[26] Winky Pinkerton, the head penguin stagehand who'd formerly worked on Broadway's *Spider-Man: Turn Off the Dark*, was verrrrry well versed in dealing with theatrical mishaps.

stage manager, who wore a curiously startled air and, of course, his green satin jacket.

"I knocked very politely," Scooter was telling them. "But they didn't answer. Do you have another way into the office, Rizzo?"

"Nope. There's just the one door, and they took the keys wit'em," said Rizzo, shrugging. *They* were obviously Statler and Waldorf.

"But golly," exclaimed Scooter, "a singer doesn't just disappear into thin air from the middle of the stage every day."

"I should think not," said Sam. "We could never afford that many understudies!"

"I guess I'll go try knocking again," said Scooter, and he hurried away.

Thereupon Pepé, the stage manager, arrived. "This ees whackadoodle. I go to make the chat with Chip to find out how the stage went dark, okay, but Chip ees nowhere to be found. Does that make any sense?" Chip was the affable if oddball IT guy in charge of all things technical at the Opera, including the lights.

"I have an announcement to make," said Sam to the others in an uncertain voice.

Pepé leaned in conspiratorially. "Are joo also terrified of the crickets?"

Sam turned and looked at the prawn, puzzled. "The announcement has nothing to do with anyone's strange insect phobias. My news is that I've sent for Inspector Fozzie Bear, who's on his way. This unsavory business needs official attention."

The stage manager shook his head at these namby-pamby milksops who remained passively parked in a corner while the whole theater was topsy-turvy. But unbeknownst to Pepé, Sam and Rizzo were not so passive as all that—they had received an order that paralyzed them; Statler and Waldorf had mysteriously told them during the last intermission that they were not to be disturbed on any account.

At that moment Scooter returned from his latest expedition. "I knocked a few times, and Statler finally opened the door," he reported. "Then he asked me the strangest thing: 'Do you have any Krazy Glue?' When I shook my head, he said, 'Well, then, beat it!' I started to tell him that something really bizarre had happened on the stage, but he just roared, 'Didn't you hear me? Krazy Glue! Find me some Krazy Glue, you blockhead!' Winky Pinkerton heard him—I mean, who didn't? He was bellowing like a bull! So Winky waddles up with a tube of glue and gives it to him. And Statler slammed the door in our faces!"

Rizzo whispered, "Betcha ten francs it's another trick of the Phantom."

Sam sighed and seemed about to speak . . . but, meeting Rizzo's eyes, said nothing. However, Sam felt his responsibility increase as the minutes passed without the managers appearing; and, at last, he could stand it no longer. "Look here, I'll go and get them out myself!"

Rizzo, turning very serious, stopped him. "Ya best be careful, Sammy! If they're stickin' to their office, it's probably because they hafta! That Phantom's got more than one trick in his bag!"

But Sam just ruffled his feathers in a huff. "If people had listened to me, the police would have known everything long ago!" And off he went.

"What's 'everything'?" asked Scooter.

"*Sí*, what ees there for to tell the police?" reiterated Pepé. "Why doan joo talk, Rizzo?" The rat was suddenly absorbed in examining his fingernails. "Ah, so joo keep quiet *porque* you know something!"

"And exactly what'm I supposed to know?"

Pepé tried to control his temper. "Just tonight, Waldorf and Statler were acting like lunatics between the acts, okay. And they woan let anyone to go near them or even to touch them!"

"Oh yeah?" Rizzo put on an innocent air.

"When I go up to Waldorf during the intermission, okay, why did Statler whisper to me, 'Go away! Whatever joo do, doan touch him!' Does he think I carry the cooties? And then Waldorf, he turns around and makes a bow, even though there ees nobody in front of him, and walks out *backward*."

Scooter's eyes widened in surprise. "Backward?"

"And Statler also walked out backward! And they went like that to the staircase leading to the managers' office: *backward*! Well, if they are not *loco*, okay, you explain what it means!"

Without much conviction, Rizzo said, "Perhaps they were practicing some a' them ballet moves?"

Pepé narrowed his eyes at the rat. "Doan be so sly, Rizzo. Joo and Sam are up to the no good."

"Whattaya mean?" asked Rizzo.

"Piggy Daaé ees not the only gone girl tonight, okay. Maybe joo can tell me why, when Mama Fiama came down to the foyer a little earlier, Sam put a wing around her and took her away with him?"

"Really?" said Rizzo as casually as possible. "I never seen it."

"Joo *did* see it—joo followed them to Sam's office, okay. Since then, joo and Sam have been seen, but no one has seen Mama Fiama."

"Whattaya think, we've eaten her or somethin'?"

"No, *porque* anyone passing by can hear her banging on the locked door and yelling, 'Let-a me at 'em, oh, let-a me at 'em!'"

Just then, Sam returned, all out of breath, tail feathers bristling. "It's worse than ever," he said in a gloomy voice. "I shouted through the door, 'Gentlemen! This is a very serious matter! Open up in the name of decency!' I heard footsteps. Waldorf finally opened the door, looking deeply distraught. He said, 'What do you want?' I answered, 'Someone has kidnapped Piggy Daaé!' And what do you think he said? *'What do you expect us to do about it?'* And he tossed me this and shut the door."

Sam held out his wing and showed them the tube of Krazy Glue.

"Maybe they were scrapbooking?" wondered Pepé. "Joo wouldn't expect it, okay, but they do like to craft."

"This is all so strange," muttered Scooter with a shiver.

"*Sí*, I find the crafting *muy* creepy, too."

"I bet none of this would be happening if my uncle J.P. was still in charge."

"Y'know, kid," said Rizzo, "to be frank with ya, he wasn't as great as all that. If you wanna know the truth, people said he was a real pain in the backside. Me, I have a much lower opinion of him."

Suddenly a voice made all three turn around. "I beg your pardon? Could you tell me where Piggy Daaé is?"

They looked to see who'd ask such a question at a time like this and saw a face so sorrow-stricken that they were at once seized with pity. It was the Vicomte Kermit de Chagny.

Pepé face-palmed. One palm after another, four times.

Chapter XV

AFTER PIGGY WENT *POOF*

Kermit's very first thought after Piggy's fantastic disappearance was that Uncle Deadly must have done it. He no longer doubted the almost supernatural powers of the pretend "Koozebanian of Music" in his domain of the Opera.

The frog rushed onto the stage in a mad fit. "Piggy! Here, Piggy, Piggy, Piggy!" he called wildly. He was certain that Deadly had discovered their secret and realized that Piggy had played him false. What vengeance would be his!

Kermit ran to the singer's dressing room. She'd told him she was going to pack light for their midnight escape, and he saw that she'd intended to keep her word: She only had fifteen suitcases and six trunks awaiting her bare necessities.

Oh, why had she refused to leave earlier?

He fumbled awkwardly at the great mirror that had once opened before his eyes to let Piggy pass through.

He pushed and pressed, but the glass apparently obeyed no one but Deadly. Perhaps actions were not enough? Perhaps he was expected to utter certain words? He tried to remember any magic commands . . .

He called out, *"Abracadabra!"*

Nothing.

"Open sesame!"

Nope.

"Bibbidi-bobbidi-boo!"

Nada.

Kermit rushed back in time to see the arriving Fozzie Bear charge onto the stage, waving and blowing kisses. "Hiya, hiya, hiya!" the inspector said, addressing the gathered throng. "What a great crowd! So let me start with a pressing question: How many actors does it take to change a lightbulb?" When no one answered, he continued. "One: The actor holds the lightbulb, and the world revolves around him! *Ba dum TSS!* Just a little showbiz humor to kick things off."

Fozzie spotted Kermit standing with Scooter, Sam, Rizzo, and Pepé. "Ah, Monsieur le Vicomte de Chagny," he said. "I've heard so much about you. I'd like to introduce myself as the finest inspector in all of France. I'd like to, but I can't! But seriously, folks, would you mind coming with me so I can ask you a few questions?"

He looked around. "Can someone show me to the office of Statler and Waldorf?"

Neither Rizzo nor Sam volunteered an answer, so Scooter told the bear that the managers had locked themselves in and knew nothing as yet of what had happened.

"Well, it's about time they found out," said Fozzie.

Sam took advantage of the moment to slip a key into Rizzo's paw. "This is all going very badly," he whispered. "You'd better let Mama Fiama out." Rizzo nodded and moved away.

As the others started ahead, Kermit felt a hand on his shoulder and heard these words spoken in his ear: "Be careful what you say about Deadly!" The frog turned around and stifled an exclamation at the sight of the fuzzy blue face with bulging eyes and a nose that looked like a curved umbrella handle. "Piggy's life depends on it!"

"But what makes you say that? And where is Piggy? And why is this chapter so short?" But the owner of the fuzzy face had already scurried off.

Chapter XVI

MAMA FIAMA'S ASTOUNDING REVELATIONS
ABOUT HER DUPLICITOUS DEALINGS

Before we follow Fozzie, I must describe certain extraordinary occurrences that had taken place in Waldorf and Statler's locked office. It involved an object about which the reader does not yet know, but which it is my duty, as an historian and avid keeper of records, to reveal without further postponement.

I have mentioned that the managers' moods had been even more disagreeable than usual, and this change was not only due to the fall of the chandelier on the infamous night of Yolanda's mooing debacle or to the nationwide shortage of prunes.

One morning a little while back, the managers had found on Statler's desk an envelope addressed to them containing a note in red ink from the Phantom. It read:

The time has come for you to deliver my

allowance. Please put twenty notes of a thousand
francs each into this envelope, seal it, and hand it
to Mama Fiama, who will do what is necessary.

I'd advise you to heed this. Don't be daft.

Ta!

Without wasting time to figure out how these
confounded communications came to show up in an
office that they were careful to keep locked, the two
men seized this opportunity to try to catch their brazen
blackmailer.

After telling the whole story in confidence to Sam
and Rizzo, they put the twenty thousand francs into the
envelope and, without asking for explanations, handed
it to Mama Fiama. She displayed no astonishment,
but went straight to the Phantom's box and placed the
precious envelope on the little shelf attached to the ledge.

The two managers, as well as Rizzo and Sam, were
hidden in such a way that they never lost sight of the
envelope for a single second the entire evening. After
the theater had emptied, they opened the still-sealed
envelope, which had not moved from the ledge.

Waldorf and Statler gasped: The twenty genuine bills

were gone and had been replaced with . . . Monopoly money! The managers' rage and fright were unmistakable. Sam wanted to send for Fozzie Bear immediately, but Waldorf said no. "We can't make ourselves look ridiculous!"

"*More* ridiculous, you mean," said Statler.

Waldorf was already thinking ahead, to the next month's allowance. "The Phantom might have won the first round, but we'll win the next one. Don't forget our old Delta Lotta Pranks fraternity slogan: 'Life, Liberty, and Always the Last Laugh.'"

We must remember that the managers still thought in the back of their minds that J.P. Grosse was continuing his practical joke. So they decided to stay patient, all the while keeping a wary eye on Mama Fiama.

"If she's a thief," said Rizzo, "that moolah is long gone."

"But, in my opinion," countered Waldorf, "she's just an idiot."

"She's not the *only* idiot in this business," said Statler.

"Without a doubt, she's showing more nerve than a root canal," said Waldorf. "Next time we'll catch her."

The next time fell on the same day that beheld the disappearance of Piggy. In the morning, a note from the Phantom reminded the two managers that the money was due. It was accompanied by the usual envelope.

They had only to insert the cash.

This was done about half an hour before the curtain rose on the first act of *Faust*. Waldorf showed the envelope to Statler, counted out the twenty thousand-franc notes in front of him, and put the bills inside, but he didn't seal it. "And now," he said, "let's trap Mama Fiama."

Rizzo fetched the old gal. She swept in wearing her black taffeta dress, the color of which, over time, had faded to rust and lilac, to say nothing of the dingy bonnet. She seemed in a good temper. "*Buonasera*, signori! It's-a for the envelope, *sì*?"

"Why yes," said Waldorf, most amiably. "For the envelope . . . and something else. Are you still on good terms with the Phantom?"

"Couldn't be better, signori."

"Well, isn't that delightful. You know," said Waldorf, leaning toward her as if to speak in confidence, "we may as well tell you, just between us all . . . you're no fool."

"Why, signori," exclaimed the box keeper, stopping the pleasant nodding of the black feathers in her bonnet, "I promise you nobody ever doubt-a that!"

"Well, since we're on the same page here, you might as well level with us: The story of the Phantom is all a big fat fib, right?"

Mama Fiama looked at the managers as though they

were speaking Swahili. She walked up to Waldorf's desk and said, rather anxiously: "I don't understand."

"Oh, we think you understand perfectly. First of all, tell us his name."

"Whose name?"

"The name of your accomplice. You do whatever he wants, right?"

"Well, he's-a not much of a bother."

"And does he still tip you?"

"You won't hear-a the complaining from me."

"How much do you get for bringing him that envelope?"

"Five or ten francs."

"You poor thing! That's not very much, is it?"

"Why?"

"We'd like to know why you have given so much to this ghost. Your friendship and devotion must be worth more than a measly five or ten francs."

"That's-a true enough. And I can tell-a you the reason, signori. It's just that . . ." She hesitated. "The Phantom, he won't like me to talk about his-a business. But . . . for you . . . I tell. It was in Box Five one evening some time ago, I find a letter addressed to me, in the red ink. I know-a this letter by heart, and I will never forget it." Mama Fiama recited the letter with unabashed pride:

"Madam:

"1839: Mademoiselle Ménétrier, leader of the ballet, becomes Marquise de Cussy.

"1848: Antoine-François de Cardevac, bass-baritone, marries to become His Royal Highness Prince Antoine-François the Duke of Västergötland.

"1861: Lola Montez, a dancer, becomes the wife of King Louis of Bavaria and is made Countess of Landsfeld.

"1977: María del Rosario Mercedes Pilar Martínez Molina Baeza, an entertainer, becomes Charo and makes an appearance on The Love Boat.*"*

Waldorf and Statler listened as the old woman enumerated these glorious turns of good fortune. And, finally, in a voice bursting with pride, she flung out the last sentence of the prophetic letter:

"Next year: Johnny Fiama, a singer, marries whomever you want him to and becomes a bona fide superstar!"

Exhausted by her impassioned recitation, the ancient usher fell into a chair, saying, "Signori, the letter was signed, 'The Phantom.' I had-a heard much of the ghost, but only half believed in him. But the day he say-a my little Johnny would be his next project, oh, I believe in him completely."

"You've never seen him, but you believe everything he says?" asked Statler.

"*Sì*. He's-a the one who get Johnny the part of Faust. He just say-a the word to signor Grosse and the thing was done."

"So Grosse saw him?"

"No, not any more than I did; but the ghost, he-a whisper in the good man's ear on that evening when he left Box Five looking molto pale."

Waldorf handed her the envelope. "Do you know what is in this?"

Mama Fiama peered into it. "Thousand-franc notes!"

"Yes, thousand-franc notes! And you already knew that! So now I'll tell you the second reason we sent for you: We are going to have you arrested!"

Surprise and indignation flashed on her face, and she advanced nearly to the nose of Waldorf, who could not help pushing back his chair. *"Have-a me arrested?!"* The mouth that spoke those words seemed to spit the few teeth it had left into Waldorf's face. The dingy bonnet swayed in menace on the old lady's tempestuous chignon.

But Waldorf retreated no farther. "That's right! I am going to have you arrested as a thief!"

And Mama Fiama gave Waldorf a mighty smack on the ear. It was not the withered hand of the angry old broad that hit the manager, but the envelope itself, the cause of all the trouble, the magic envelope that opened with the blow, scattering the francs, which escaped in a fantastic whirl like giant butterflies.

"A *thief*?" She choked with rage, shouting, "How dare-a you!" And suddenly, she darted up to Waldorf again. "In any case," she growled, "you, signor Waldorf, ought to know better than I where the money went to!"

"And how should I know?" asked Waldorf, astounded.

"Because the francs went into *your pocket*!" gasped the old woman, looking at Waldorf as if he were the devil incarnate.

He would have tackled Mama Fiama if Statler had not quickly asked her, more gently, "How can you suspect my dear old fraternity brother of putting twenty thousand francs in his pocket?"

"I never said that," declared Mama Fiama, "seeing that it was I *myself* who sneak-a the twenty thousand francs into signor Waldorf's pocket." And she added, under her breath, "The secret is out! And may the Phantom forgive-a me!"

"I'm lost," said Statler.

"The envelope that Waldorf give-a me was the one that I slipped into Waldorf's pocket," explained Mama Fiama. "The one that I took to the ghost's box was *another* envelope, one that look-a just like it, which the ghost give-a me beforehand and which I slipped up my sleeve."

And Mama Fiama took from her sleeve an envelope identical to the one that contained the twenty thousand francs and passed it to the managers. They opened it. It contained twenty Monopoly bills like those that had astounded them the month before.

"How simple!" said Waldorf and Statler at the same time. "Jinx—you owe me a Coke!" they added in tandem.

"So," summarized Statler, "the ghost gave you this envelope and told you to substitute it for the one that we gave you? And it was the ghost who told you to put the other one into Waldorf's pocket?"

"Yes, it was-a the ghost. He tell-a me to slip it in your pocket when you don't expect it."

"Well, I'll be! Never felt a thing!" exclaimed Waldorf. "It's devilishly clever!"

"Oh, it's clever, no doubt!" Statler agreed. "Only you forget, Waldorf, dear old chum, that ten thousand francs of the twenty were *mine*, and nothing ended up in *my* pocket!"

Chapter XVII

HOW THE TWO USED THE GLUE

Statler's suspicions irked Waldorf, but he agreed to put up with his partner's wishes for the time being, if only to discover the good-for-nothing who was ripping them off.

This brings us to that night's first intermission, with the strange behavior between them observed by Pepé. Waldorf and Statler had decided to backtrack, walking through everything they'd done on the night the first twenty thousand francs disappeared. Statler would trail his partner and not for a single second lose sight of Waldorf's coat pocket, into which Mama Fiama was to slip the twenty thousand francs, just as she'd done before.

Waldorf went and placed himself at the exact spot where he had stood in the lobby that first fateful night. Statler took up his position a few steps behind him.

Mama Fiama passed, bumped up against Waldorf, dropped her envelope of twenty thousand francs into his coat pocket . . . and, according to part of the plan she knew nothing about, promptly found herself guided with alacrity by Sam Eagle into his office. There, he locked the furious usher inside, thus making it impossible for her to have any communication with the Phantom.

Meanwhile, Waldorf was bending and bowing and walking backward, just as he had when he'd greeted those bigwig donors in front of him. He bowed . . . to nobody and walked backward . . . before nobody . . . And he continued to do so all the way to the offices of the management. Constantly watched by Statler from behind, he kept an eye out for anyone approaching from the front.

Two minutes later, they locked themselves in their office. Statler put the key in his pocket. "We stayed locked up like this last time," he said, "until you left the Opera to go home."

"Right. And nobody bothered us?"

"*Everyone* bothers us."

"But that night we didn't see anyone, did we?" said Waldorf, who was trying to think back. "Why don't you help by using that photographic memory of yours—or did you forget to take off the lens cap?"

Statler chuckled, then shook his head. "I guess I must have been robbed on my way home from the Opera."

"No," said Statler in a drier tone than ever, "that's

impossible. I took you there in a cab. The twenty thousand francs disappeared at your place: There's no doubt about that."

"Statler, I've had enough of your suspicion!"

"Waldorf, I've had too much of it!"

"So you're accusing me of something?"

"Yes, of a silly joke!"

"Who jokes with twenty thousand francs?"

"You tell me," declared Statler, opening up a magazine and ostentatiously studying its contents. "We'll just sit here till we leave to go home."

Waldorf plucked the magazine from Statler's hands. "Look here," he said, "it's just as possible that the twenty thousand francs disappeared from my coat pocket when I left the cab we rode in together."

"What are you implying?" asked Statler, crimson with rage.

"You were the only one near me, so if the twenty thousand francs was no longer in my pocket, it stood a pretty good chance of being in *yours*. See? There's more than one way to think about this sticky situation."

Statler leaped up at the suggestion. "Sticky!" he shouted, raising a finger into the air. *"Krazy Glue!"*

"Krazy Glue?"

"Let's get a tube!"

"Have you totally lost it? What for?"

"To fasten you up with!"

"You want to fasten me up with Krazy Glue?"

"Yes, to attach you to the twenty thousand francs! Then, whether it's here, or on the cab ride to your place, or at your place, you'll feel the hand that pulls at your pocket, and you'll see if it's mine!"

And that was the moment when Statler opened the door to the passage and shouted, "Krazy Glue! Somebody give me some Krazy Glue!" And we also know how Winky Pinkerton then delivered the tube. Statler locked the door again, then he knelt down next to Waldorf.

Statler took the envelope from his friend's pocket and removed the cash—all the bills were there, all quite genuine. He put them back in the envelope and the envelope back in the jacket pocket, and glued it to the lining. Then he sat down next to Waldorf and kept his eyes fixed on him, while Waldorf, sitting at his desk, didn't stir.

"Now let's just wait," said Statler. "We only have a few minutes till the clock strikes twelve. Last time, we left at the last stroke."

The time passed, slow and heavy. Waldorf tried to laugh. "Feels kinda strange in here, doesn't it?"

"Yeah," said Statler, who was starting to feel squirmy.

"The ghost!" continued Waldorf in a low voice, as though fearing he might be overheard by invisible ears. "What if it is a ghost who puts the magic envelopes on the table . . . who talks in Box Five . . . who squished Beauregard . . . who unhooked the chandelier . . . and who robs us! I mean, there's no one here except you and me, and if the cash disappears and neither of us has anything to do with it, well, we'll have to believe in the Phantom, won't we."

At that moment, the clock on the mantelpiece gave its warning click. A bird popped out of the door of the wooden home and, at the first stroke of twelve, called *cuckoo*! Eleven more followed. As the winged timekeeper prepared to return into the clock, she eyed the two grouches and muttered under her breath, *"You're both cuckoo . . ."* Then she disappeared, her door clicking shut.

The managers shuddered in the stillness that followed. Perspiration formed on their foreheads. They gave a sigh and eased themselves up out of their chairs. Statler suggested that he take a look in Waldorf's pocket, and boy oh boy, was he not happy with what he found— or, rather, *didn't*.

Waldorf slipped out of his coat. The two managers turned the pocket inside out: The envelope was still glued to the pocket, but all the bills were gone!

Chapter XVIII

THE VISCOUNT FACES FOZZIE

66**I** tried acting once," the police inspector Fozzie Bear was saying when he entered the managers' office. "I really moved the audience—everyone left after the first act! Wocka wocka! But speaking of people who've disappeared . . ." Then he broke the news to Statler and Waldorf about how the prima donna went missing so mysteriously.

"I can't believe it," said Waldorf, dropping his head into his hands. "Right in the middle of the show? It's enough to make a guy resign!" And he pulled a few hairs out of his mustache without even knowing what he was doing.

Statler added, chagrined, "This is certain to wind up in the papers."

"You know what else makes headlines?" asked Fozzie. "Corduroy pillows."

Just then Kermit announced, "I can tell you the name

of the creature that carried off Piggy, and I can tell you where he lives . . . when we're alone." Fozzie got his drift and invited Kermit to take a seat. He cleared the room of everyone except the frog and the managers.

Kermit took a deep breath and began, "He is called Uncle Deadly, he lives in a carnival in the underground cellars of the Opera, and he is the Koozebanian of Music!"

Fozzie was surprised. "A Koozebanian! From the planet Koozebane?" Turning to the managers, Fozzie asked, "Do you have any extraterrestrials on your payroll?"

Waldorf and Statler shook their heads.

"Oh," said Kermit, "they may know him as 'the Phantom of the Opera.' The Phantom and the Koozebanian of Music are the same person. And his real name is Uncle Deadly."

Fozzie Bear rose and looked at the managers. "Gentlemen, it appears that you know a phantom?"

Waldorf rose, still holding the remaining hairs of his mustache. "No, we do not, but we wish that we did, because just tonight he robbed us of twenty thousand francs!"

Fozzie looked at the managers, then back at Kermit, and wondered whether he had wandered into a lunatic asylum. He took off his hat and passed a hand along the top of his fuzzy head.

Statler peered skeptically at the frog. "You've actually *seen* this Deadly fellow?"

"Yes," Kermit said, "in a cemetery."

Fozzie didn't seem surprised. "A cemetery is a great place to come up with a story—there are so many plots there."

"Look," said Kermit, "I know this must sound crazy. But you have to believe that I'm not bonkers. The safety of the person I care about most in the world is at stake. Every minute is valuable—but, unfortunately, if I don't tell you the strangest story that ever was, and from the very beginning, you won't believe me."

So Kermit shared the whole wild tale. And although Statler and Waldorf had hoped to learn some detail that would reveal their hoaxer, they were soon compelled to accept the fact that Monsieur Viscount Kermit de Chagny, with his story about blue-tailed creatures and enchanted hurdy-gurdies, was completely off his rocker.

When Kermit's story was done, Fozzie said, "I've a few more questions for you, if you don't mind. You had planned to run off with Piggy tonight, correct?"

"Yes."

"After the performance?"

"Yes."

"All your arrangements were made?"

"Yes."

"And you have a carriage outside?"

"Yes, yes, yes! Can we go already?"

"Did you know that there were three other carriages there, in addition to yours?"

"I didn't pay any attention."

"Well, they were carriages for Janice Sorelli; for Yolanda; and for your brother, Constantine. But only Constantine's is gone."

"I'm not sure what you're getting at . . ."

"Constantine didn't want you to run off with Piggy, right?"

"I'm sorry, but that's none of your beeswax."

"Okay, then, you've answered my question: He didn't want you to be together . . . and that was why you were taking her away from Paris? Well, Kermit, I hate to tell you, but I think your brother has betrayed you! Right after Piggy's disappearance, he dashed into his carriage and they bolted across the city."

"Ahhhhhhhhhh," cried the frog, waving his spindly arms in the air frantically, "I've got to catch them!" And he rushed out of the office.

When Kermit had gone, Fozzie confessed to Statler and Waldorf that he had no idea if Constantine had run away with Piggy or not. But planting the idea in Kermit's head meant that the younger frog would do all the footwork necessary to discover whether his brother was a suspect. Fozzie tapped his temple with pride and said, "I invented this concept. I'm calling it outsourcing."[27]

But the inspector would not have been quite so satisfied with himself if he had known that his unwitting deputy was stopped at the entrance to the very first corridor after he left the managers' office. The figure who blocked his way said, "Where are you rushing off to?"

"It's you!" Kermit said. "Who *are* you, anyway?"

"You know who I am! I am the Great Gonzo! And you're standing on my cape."

---

[27] This tactic also allowed Fozzie to depart the theater in time to make open-mic night at Le Chuckle Room.

Chapter XIX

BADLY DRESSED FOR SUCCESS

The guy with the blue fur, oversize eyes, and dramatic cape said to Kermit, "No one in the world but Deadly could pull off a disappearing act like that! Now let's go find him."

Kermit balked. "The inspector said Piggy has been whisked away by my brother!"

"Look, don't say I said this, because he's realllly sensitive, but Fozzie's police skills are even worse than his jokes. Constantine would never do that."

"Somehow I trust you already—maybe it's because you're the only one who won't look at me like I'm loopy when I mention Deadly."

At the sound of that name, Kermit felt Gonzo grab him with hands that were so cold, they'd certainly be blue if they weren't already.

"Zip it!" said Gonzo in an urgent hiss, then he cocked an ear and listened to the distant sounds of the theater.

"We should never mention his name here. So we don't attract his attention, let's just say 'he,' or 'whatshisname,' or 'Linda.'"

"All right. But do you think . . . *Linda* is nearby?"

"He may be, but he's probably with Piggy right now at the carnival on the lake."

"So you know about the carnival, too?"

Nodding, Gonzo continued, "If he's not there, he may be here, in this wall, in this floor, in this ceiling!" As they walked on and reached the intersection of another hallway, Gonzo peered in both directions. "I wonder where Quongo is . . ."

"Who's Quongo?"

"My servant. Let's go this way!"

Stealthy Gonzo led Kermit down passages that he'd never seen before, even when Piggy would take him for one of her endless walks throughout the building. As they moved, Gonzo asked in the softest of whispers, "How much did you tell Fozzie?"

"I told him that Piggy's abductor was the Koozebanian of Music, aka the Phantom of the Opera, and that his real name was Uncle—"

"*Ixnay!*" Gonzo cut him off. "And did he believe you?"

"No."

"Perfect!" said Gonzo.

After going up and down several staircases, through a long tunnel, along a balance beam, and up a salmon ladder—Kermit asked at one point, "Are we looking for Piggy or auditioning for *Paris Ninja Warrior?*"—the two eventually found themselves in front of Piggy's dressing-room door. "Wow, you really know the ins and outs of this building."

"Not as well as Linda does," said Gonzo with a foreboding look. "We can change in there."

"Change? Into what?"

Gonzo left the question unanswered and ushered the young frog into the dressing room, which was exactly as Kermit had left it some minutes earlier. Except for the giant gorilla eating a banana. "Quongo! Perfect timing," said Gonzo, closing the door behind them.

The gorilla handed Gonzo a suitcase and started to go. But Gonzo stopped him. "Wait—I'll take your banana peel, too. You never know when something like that might come in handy. One time I used avocados and a picket-fence post to make a skateboard. Too bad it filled the halfpipe with guacamole." Quongo passed him the peel and plodded out of the room, barely squeezing his massive body through the doorframe.

"Wow, that Quongo is a little on the heavy side."

"Fair to say he's heavy on *every* side," said Gonzo. He opened the case. It was stuffed full of some truly terrible fashions: polyester shirts with giant collars, paisley-printed bell-bottom pants, a puka shell necklace. "When Piggy vanished, I sent word to Quongo to bring these. I've been stocking up because they're the best way to battle He Who Must Not Be Named," said Gonzo.

Kermit whispered, "How can clothes defeat him?"

"He's very offended by bad fashion. His mentor, Mr. Poodlepants, gave him a taste for style, and now it actually makes him physically weak to see anything atrocious. Go on, pick out the craziest combo you can find, and let's get changed."

"Wow, these are really something," said Kermit, sorting through the options. "Do we really have to?"

"Think of Piggy. You really care about her, don't you?"

"I worship the ground she tromps on! But why would *you* risk *your* life for her? You must really despise He Who Must Not Be Named."

"No," said Gonzo in a melancholy voice, "I don't despise him. I actually feel sorry for him."

"That sounds just like her . . ."

Gonzo didn't reply. After putting on a mauve velour tracksuit, a ten-gallon cowboy hat, and orange Crocs with loud socks ("so my feet won't fall asleep"), he slipped the banana peel into his right front pocket. He fetched a stool and set it against the wall facing the huge mirror. Then he climbed onto the stool and, with his nose to the pineapple-print wallpaper, seemed to be looking for something. "Ah," he said, after a long search, "there it is!" And, reaching up, he pressed against a corner in the pattern of the paper. Then he did a somersault off the stool and grabbed a little lantern off the table.

Kermit was now dressed in argyle clamdiggers and a mesh tank top.

"Wow, you look *terrible*," pronounced Gonzo, clearly pleased. Then he gave a gentle push against the mirror. "It takes some time to release the counterbalance that pivots the wall."

"How did Linda know about all of these tricks?"

"He built them!"

Suddenly, in a blinding daze of crosslights, the mirror turned like a revolving door, carrying the uniquely clad Kermit and Gonzo with it, hurling them from full light into the deepest darkness.

Chapter XX

SETTING OUT INTO THE CELLARS

The wall behind them finished its full circle and closed again. They stood motionless in the gloom and silence, till Gonzo suddenly exclaimed, "Well, *that* rocked! Let's do it again?"

"There's no time!"

"Drat, you're right." He turned up the flame of his lantern. They could now see that the floor, walls, and ceiling were all formed of wood planking. It must have been the secret passage that Deadly used to reach Piggy's dressing room.

Gonzo set the light on the ground and slipped to his furry knees, feeling around for something on the floor. Kermit heard a faint click, then watched as a very pale luminous square appeared like a window on the dimly lit level below.

Gonzo whispered, "Follow me and do everything that I do." Holding on to the edge, he let his body hang into the opening. Then he let go, executing a forward double-somersault, three-and-a-half-twist pike position drop into the darkness.

"Um, you do you," Kermit whispered down to Gonzo, "I'll do me."

"Suit yourself," came Gonzo's voice from below, "but my way is a lot more exciting! I once did the same move from five stories up into a hot tub filled with cheese curds. Boy, was that a mistake."

"Why? Did you break something?"

"No, but I learned the hard way that I'm verrrry lactose intolerant."

Kermit dropped the lantern down to his guide. Then he closed his eyes and let himself fall. Gonzo caught him, softening his landing. He started to ask a question, but Gonzo covered his mouth as they heard a voice, which they recognized as that of Fozzie Bear.

Kermit and Gonzo were completely hidden behind a wooden partition. Near them, a small staircase led to the door of a little room in which the police inspector seemed to be pacing and asking questions of someone. The faint light was just enough to enable Kermit to distinguish the shape of things around him. And he couldn't restrain a startled *ribbit*: there was a *corpse* lying on the narrow landing against the door at the top of the staircase!

Gonzo had also seen the body, and he involuntarily whispered one word in explanation: *"Linda!"*

Fozzie's voice was now heard more distinctly. He was asking the stage manager for information about the theatrical lighting system. It was normally operated by Chip from the booth just below the stage where they were talking. But Chip apparently wasn't in his usual place, and no one had seen the techie since right before curtain time, when he was spotted in the wings writing "code" on a "laptop" for something he was inventing called "Pong."

Someone pushed at the door that opened onto the little staircase, but due to the body blocking it, it didn't get very far. "Wow," they heard Pepé marvel, "ees this always so difficult, okay, or are my barre classes not paying off?"

Next, they saw Fozzie wedge the door open a bit with his shoulder. He caught a glimpse of what was stopping its progress. "Uh-oh."

"What ees it?" asked Pepé.

"I think it's a sack of potatoes disguised as a person," said Fozzie, then he shook his head. "That can't be right."

"Why not?" asked Pepé.

"Because the only food that gets dressed is salad. Wocka wocka!"

Pepé peered around the bear to get a look at the lump. He recognized the face at once: "Chip! *Ay caramba!* He ees dead, okay. And that ees not okay!"

Fozzie pointed at a pile of empty wrappers that lay near the prone IT guy. "I actually think," he announced, "that your colleague may be in a sugar coma."

Dr. Honeydew soon arrived and confirmed Fozzie's initial diagnosis: "A severe case of hypersugaritis. It appears he consumed so many candy bars that his insulin level spiked and then crashed harder than a hang-gliding hippo. He's fallen into a deep, unconscious sleep."

"Very curious!" said the inspector. "Somebody must have wanted Chip out of the way, and that person was obviously working with the kidnapper—or maybe it was *actually* the kidnapper *himself.*"

Thereupon, Kermit and Gonzo saw the startled faces of Statler and Waldorf appear in the doorway. Statler frowned. "Somebody better get to the bottom of this, and frankly I don't have a lot of faith in this bear's brains."

"Yeah," added Waldorf, "a mind reader would only charge him half price!"

The two managers disappeared.

"Jeez," said Fozzie to Pepé, "I know I'm not great at this job, but I stay awake nights trying to figure out how to do it better. Now if only I could stay awake days!"

The stage manager, holding his chin with four hands in an attitude of profound thought, said, "Joo know, it ees not the first time that Chip has done the sugary snoozing. I remember finding him down here another night, okay, out cold with a whole bunch of the candy wrappers beside him."

"When was that?" asked Fozzie, carefully jotting something in his notebook.

"*Actualmente*," said Pepé with a snap of the fingers, "it was the night that Yolanda made the sound like the cow." Encouraged, he asked the inspector, "Joo are taking notes?"

"Oh, no, but I *am* working on jokes *about* notes—*musical* notes! I'm starting my own humor website. I'm going to call it WockaWockapedia. Let me try these new ones out on you: Why was the musician arrested?"

The prawn shrugged.

"Because he was in *treble*! See, it's a pun. Or what about this one: What musical note can stop an eighteen-wheeler? Give up? *A flat*!" Pepé was silent. Fozzie nodded: "All right, so we'll call that two maybes."

Kermit and Gonzo, still unseen, watched as a group of sheep arrived to cart out the still-sleeping Chip. Fozzie and the others departed, as well.

When they were alone again, Gonzo waved for Kermit

to follow. As they progressed along the dark passageways, both seemed lost in thought.

Kermit wondered what he would have done without such an expert guide in this extraordinary labyrinth . . .

Gonzo wondered if mothballs would be a good substitute for cheese curds . . .

They had just reached the third cellar when suddenly a fantastic face came in sight down the dark passage—a whole fiery face, not just two glowing eyes! Yes, *a head of fire* was moving toward them, seemingly floating a few feet off the ground.

"What in the name of Evel Knievel is that?!" marveled Gonzo, between his teeth. "I guess Seymour the fireman wasn't hallucinating, after all. It reminds me of the time I juggled tiki torches while tightroping along dental floss over the flaming mouth of Mount Vesuvius. Boy was it hot. And boy was using *waxed* floss a big mistake."

Kermit was transfixed by the flaming visage that approached. "Is that Linda?"

"I doubt it, but whatever it is, he may have sent it."

They began to perceive a certain noise of which they could not guess the nature. It seemed to be approaching along with the fiery face. It sounded as though thousands of nails were being scraped against a blackboard.

They slowly backed away, but the fiery face—orange

in complexion, with a shaggy mane of fuchsia hair—advanced, gaining on them fast. The eyes were round and staring from beneath bushy black brows, the nose like a red golf ball; a gaping mouth revealed a bottom row of ferocious white teeth. It seemed to be chanting one word over and over, but they couldn't quite make out what it was saying.

How did that blazing face manage to glide through the darkness? And how did it go so fast, so straight ahead, with such unblinking eyes? And what was that scratching, scraping, grating sound that it brought with it?

Gonzo and Kermit flattened themselves against the wall, not knowing what was going to happen because of that incomprehensible head of fire, and especially now, because of the hundreds of little sounds that moved in the darkness, under the fiery face. And it kept chanting . . . chanting . . . saying something like . . .

Nope, still too hard to make out.

The two companions, flat against the wall, soon knew what the thousand noises meant: It was a troop, hustled along in the shadows in innumerable little hurried waves, swifter than the waves that rush over the sands at high tide, under the fiery head that was like a bloodred moon. And the little waves reached the gents and climbed up their legs.

Rats! They were rats!

Kermit and Gonzo squirmed and struggled to contain themselves—not because they were terrified, as most would be, but because they were verrrry ticklish, and those cute little rat feet were making them giggle.

Now they could clearly hear what the head of fire was chanting: "AN-I-MAL! AN-I-MAL! AN-I-MAL!" It heard their laughter and spoke to them: "S'mores! Animal make s'mores! Rats love s'mores!" They could now see that he was holding several skewers of flaming marshmallows, the source of the flickering light that illuminated his face. Next to him, a rat in tattered clothes carrying several chocolate bars said, "Hey, brahs, wanna join us? We're going out to buy more graham crackers at the Sept-Onze on the corner."

"Oh, gee, thanks," said Kermit, barely recovered from his tickle-induced giggles, "but we're actually on a mission of our own."

"All right, but man, you're missing out. This Animal guy makes killer s'mores. If you change your mind, find us in the second cellar. We built a supercool rec room with a foosball table. If you see my cousin Rizzo, tell him we'll be kickin' it in there all night!"

The head of fire started up a new chant—"CrackERS! CrackERS! CrackERS!"—and on the excited gang went up the passage till they vanished and the darkness returned.

"Is the lake far from here?" Kermit asked Gonzo. "When we get there, we can call out and Piggy will hear us! And *he* will hear us, too! And, since you're tight with him, we'll persuade him to come to his senses!"

"Slow your roll, pardner," said Gonzo. "We'll never enter the fun house on the lake by going *across* the lake! He'll know we're coming. We have to surprise him."

They continued their journey and gradually arrived at what appeared to be a storage area. Making their way among all manner of set pieces, they reached a row of twenty-foot-high scenery flats stacked on their ends like books slotted onto a shelf. Between two scenes from *Death in Venice* there was just enough room for a body to pass through . . . like the body that one day not long ago was found squished there: the body of Beauregard.

Fearlessly, Gonzo slipped through, with Kermit close upon his heels. "This is just stretched canvas," said a perplexed Gonzo as he felt the flat with his hand. "How could anyone be squished by something with so much *give* to it? Hmm, doesn't really make sense. Beauregard must have been squished somewhere else, then brought here to be discovered . . ."

With his free hand, he felt the brick wall beyond the

flats. Kermit saw him push on it in various spots, just as he had pressed on the pineapple wallpaper in Piggy's dressing room. Finally, a large stone gave way and a narrow hole opened in the wall!

Gonzo wiggled through but stopped almost at once. Kermit heard him feeling the stones farther along inside the passage. Then Gonzo lifted the dim lantern again to examine something on the floor. Kermit heard him whisper, "Great news! We'll have to drop down to *another* level! So here's the plan: I'm going to execute an arm-stand back-double-somersault with one-and-a-half twists. Then you'll do exactly the same. Or, okay, fine— you do you. Don't look so worried! I'll catch you again. And these very arms once caught a two-hundred-pound ball of cookie dough shot from a cannon on top of the Empire State Building."

Kermit next heard two things: a dull thud below him, evidently produced by Gonzo's landing, and then, behind him, the quiet scrape of the stone through which they'd entered the passage as it slid back into place. Gonzo whispered from below: "Deadly has rigged all the stones to close by themselves!"

There was no turning back now. "Well, here goes nothing," muttered Kermit, and he dropped down into Gonzo's outstretched arms.

"You know something," said Gonzo after he caught him, "you might be a lot less slippery than cookie dough, but you're a lot more clammy."

They stood motionless in this unknown new space, listening. The darkness was thick, the silence heavy and terrible.

Then Gonzo lifted the lantern. The light swept along the wall and all around them. It was difficult at first to make out the appearance of things. Then they saw that the beams of light seemed to reflect themselves . . .

Kermit passed his hand over that reflection, and his one hand turned to two. "Goodness gracious," he exclaimed.

"It's a mirror," said Gonzo, concerned. "And there are hundreds more all around us! I don't want to be a Negative Nancy, but we may never find our way out!"

What Gonzo knew of this reflective labyrinth and what there befell him and his companion shall be told in his own words, as set down in a manuscript that he left behind him, and which I copy verbatim.[28]

---

[28] People *really* liked to keep journals back in the day.

Chapter XXI

THE INTERESTING AND INSTRUCTIVE
VICISSITUDES OF A DETERMINED DAREDEVIL

From Gonzo's Journal

So—finally!—I, the Great Gonzo, managed to enter the carnival on the lake. Just not exactly how I'd hoped to do it.

As a daredevil and lifetime member of OOPSIE (the Organization of Professional Stunt-Incline Experts), I've always been a sucker for thrill rides and getting all dizzy and disoriented inside fun houses. And when it came to creating them, Deadly was the best in the biz. How many times I'd begged the "Midway Madman" to let me experience his ultimate creation. But he always blew me off.

Despite all that, I didn't give up trying to get inside. Once I even strapped fifty industrial-strength pogo sticks to my legs, but those stones were waaay stronger than the springs—and my skull. I really should invest in a helmet one of these days.

I tried to spy on him to see how he worked the trick door in the wall, but it was just too dark down there. Moving around underground was second nature to him by now. He was like a bat—he barely needed light. (And also, he loved fruit juice and might have had rabies. Unconfirmed.)

One day not long before Kermit and I finally made our way inside, I got the idea to swim across the lake. But before I jumped in, I saw about a dozen shark fins cutting the surface: He'd stocked the water with great whites!

Of course, sharks in the water only made the challenge more tempting for me—but wouldn't you know it, I'd *just* dropped off my shark-proof suit at the dry cleaner's. As I stood there trying to think of an alternative, Deadly emerged from the shadows, his legs pumping a little swan-shaped paddleboat at a snail's pace across the water.

"How irritating you are, Gonzo!" he hollered out. The swan finally nudged onto the shore, and Deadly stepped out. "Did you save my life only to show up and constantly annoy me?"

"I'm glad you brought that up: I *did* save your life, and you owe me big-time. If I hadn't drained the log ride track, you would be dead as a doornail."

See, many years before, in a carnival outside Reykjavik, Deadly was performing in the sideshow.

He'd been discovered by Mr. Poodlepants, a pioneering carnival entrepreneur with a flair for visuals. Poodlepants costumed Deadly in a fine brocade jacket and put a burlap sack over his terrifying head. He exhibited Deadly as "The Dapper Draped Dragon" and had him sing for admiring crowds, because, irony of ironies, his voice was as beautiful as his face was fearsome. I happened to catch his act while passing through Iceland scouting for the perfect waterfall to sail over inside a butter churn.

There weren't a lot of us blue types around, so we struck up a sort of odd friendship. I found out that looking like he did had given him a hard demeanor, but when it came to women, he was a total softie. And he was an absolute sucker for romance.

Now, Mean Mama was a fellow sideshow performer whose act—bench-pressing cannonballs while lying on a bed of nails—followed the Dapper Draped Dragon's. Despite the fact that she looked like a cross between a radioactive rabbit and a gargantuan grizzly, Deadly found her monstrously cute.

But Mean Mama was already married to the very possessive Big Mean Carl, who, also being part of the genus *Meanus*, looked a lot like Mean Mama, though he was bigger and hungrier. He once consumed a whole herd of wildebeest just because he thought one of them had given him the side-eye.

One night, Deadly dared to leave a dozen roses for Mean Mama in her tent, and Carl discovered them. He was furious. He devoured the flowers, then he chased Deadly all around the fairgrounds, threatening to eat him, as well.

With Carl gaining on him, Deadly reached the flume ride and boarded one of the log-shaped boats. Off he went. Carl squeezed his hulking bulk into the next one, yelling the entire time that as soon as he caught Deadly, he was going to gobble him up.

Luckily for Deadly, all the logs traveled the ride's splashy curves, climbs, and drops at the same speed. When his log reached the end of the ride, I was waiting with a brilliant plan: As soon as he stepped back onto land, I pulled the track's plug and drained the water from the ride's entire trough, stranding Carl well short of the finish and letting Deadly escape with his life. He fled that carnival fast, eventually making his way to England, where he picked up his posh accent, and then finally to France in the wake of Brexit.

Sadly, in the end, Mean Mama rejected her would-be suitor, saying that his face was too scary even for her. Eventually that callus-backed heartbreaker left Big Mean

Carl and the carnival life altogether, and now works as a mattress tester for Macy's.

"Have you quite finished with your exposition?" asked Deadly, standing impatiently on the shore of the lake.

"Can't promise that," I told him. "There are still eight pages left in this chapter."

He boarded the swan boat and said, "However much he may appreciate the favor you have done him, Deadly may in the end forget it; and you know that nothing can restrain Deadly, not even Deadly himself. Especially when Deadly talks about Deadly in the third person." He bicycle-paddled at a crawl back toward the other side of the lake.

The next day—

"Still paddling here!" Deadly shouted from the shadows. "Don't rush me!" I waited till, finally, he was gone.

So, as I was saying, wouldn't you know, the next day I found out the dry cleaner's lost my shark-proof suit. It's the Murphy's Law of daredeviling. (Not the one you're thinking. This one came from Lavinia Murphy, the founder of OOPSIE and a fount of wisdom, who said that the readiness of your equipment for a stunt is often in inverse proportion to your mental resolve to execute said stunt.)

There just *had* to be another way into the carnival. I'd

often seen Deadly disappear from the third cellar, though I couldn't imagine how he was pulling it off. So from the hallway outside Piggy's dressing room, I eavesdropped on his singing lessons with her. I heard him warble those fantastic tunes that I later came to find out had hypnotized the singer. But, all the same, I would never have thought that Deadly's voice, no matter how good it was, could make her not be scared of his looks. *Everyone* was scared of his looks. But then it all clicked when I learned that Piggy hadn't actually *seen* him!

Late one night I slipped into her dressing room. After about nine hours and thirteen-and-a-half cups of cold brew I finally discovered the trick that made the wall spin around. And a few days later, I followed that passage down into the cellars and encountered Deadly, cloaked in black, standing there with both Piggy, who was slumped on the ground—Deadly had clearly sung her into a stupor—and the camel that had disappeared from the stables, kneeling and chewing its cud. It was like the weirdest nativity scene ever.

So I went to help. Bad idea! He was furious to see me, and before I had time to say a word, he conked me on the noggin and knocked me out cold.

When I came to, I touched my head: A big goose egg had shown up (so cool!), but Deadly, Piggy, and the camel had disappeared. I knew that the poor pig was now a prisoner in Deadly's crazy carnival. (So *not* cool.)

I beelined to the banks of the lake. For twenty-four hours I kept a lookout, waiting for Deadly to show himself and playing sudoku. Eventually I heard a little splashing in the dark. I saw the two green eyes shining like creepy candles about ten yards away, and forty-five minutes later the swan inched to shore.

Deadly jumped out and walked up to me. "I have *got* to get a faster boat," he muttered, puffing and blowing like a walrus. "And you, Gonzo! You've been here for a day and a night, and you're vexing me. Deadly spared you yesterday, but I warn you, don't let Deadly catch you here again!"

He was so furious that I didn't think, for the moment, of butting in. "You're being reckless," he continued. "Someone will end up wondering what you are after here, and they will end up knowing that you are after Deadly. And then they will be after Deadly themselves and they will discover my carnival on the lake! If they do, it will be bad luck for you. If Deadly's secrets cease to be Deadly's secrets, *it will be bad luck for the lot of you*, nincompoop!" He sat down on the stern of his swan and kicked his heels against it, waiting.

I simply said, "It's not you that I'm after."

He retorted, "I have every right to entertain her in my

own fun house. For I have been *truly seen and not feared*."

"Oh poo, that's not true," I said. "You've mesmerized her, and you're keeping her locked up."

"Listen here, furball," he said. "If I prove that you're wrong, will you promise never to meddle in my affairs again?"

"You betcha," I said without hesitation, because I didn't think that was possible.

"Well, then, it's quite simple. Piggy Daaé shall leave the fun house as she pleases and come back again! Yes, she'll come back again, because she has *truly seen me and not been afraid*! Deadly has changed!"

I couldn't help but feel sad when I thought of how he viewed himself as a monster. We had a lot in common: I knew what it was like to be an oddity. We were both blue. We made people uneasy, or worse. I mean, we might as well have come from Koozebane. I'd learned how to fit in enough to get by (rule #1: If someone invites you over to "chill," don't show up with a truckload of ice cubes). But he thought he was too scary to be accepted as part of humanity—and humanity pretty much confirmed this thinking.

"Fine," I told him. "I'll believe you if I see Piggy leave the carnival and then choose to go back."

"And you won't bother Deadly anymore?"

"Nope."

"Goodie. Then go to the Opera tonight. After the masquerade ball, you'll see Piggy completely chuffed to come back down and visit me."

To my shock, things happened pretty much as he said they would. Piggy left the carnival and returned to it several times, and it didn't seem like she was being forced to do anything. I kept my promise to stay away from the shore of the lake . . . But the idea of that secret entrance to the third cellar never left my brain.

I went and waited for hours at a time, hoping to learn how Deadly opened it—and my patience was rewarded. One day, I watched as he went between the two scenery flats. I tiptoed closer and saw as he pressed on a spring that opened a secret door in the stone. He slipped through, and the stone closed behind him. Hallelujah!

I counted to fifty Mississippi, then opened the stone myself. Everything happened as it had when Deadly pressed it—*sahweet*! But since I knew Deadly was in there somewhere, I didn't go any farther. I figured I'd wait to explore it at a safer time, so I left the cellars after carefully making sure the stone was back in place.

In the period that followed, I continued to wander, very cautiously, around the Opera. I was nervous about what he might be up to. Oh, I wasn't worried for myself—

this body is pretty much unbreakable, and believe me, I've tried. I was worried for everyone else.

Deadly kept Piggy dependent on him with their lessons, but it was clear that the pig's heart belonged to the Vicomte Kermit de Chagny. While they frolicked about like an innocent engaged couple on the upper floors and roof of the Opera to avoid Deadly, they never suspected that someone besides Elvis was watching over them. But that someone was me! I was prepared to do anything to protect them.

Meanwhile, Deadly never showed himself. I wish that had made me feel better . . .

Still, I had a plan: I thought that Deadly's jealousy over Kermit would lure him out of the carnival, giving me the opening to slip in safely through the trapdoor in the third cellar. It was important for everybody's sake that I learn exactly what was down there.

One day, tired of waiting for an opportunity, I chanced it and moved the stone. From below I could hear music: Deadly was composing. I was careful not to make any noise as I listened in.

He stopped playing his hurdy-gurdy for a moment, and it sounded like he was pacing around like a madman. He bellowed, "'The Storm Cloud Connection' must be finished *first*! Quite finished!"

"First"? *Then* what? I wondered what he was planning. When he started playing again, I closed the stone very softly.

On the night of Piggy Daaé's disappearance, I didn't go to the theater until pretty late in the evening. I'd been searching Paris all day for the perfect plungers in preparation for my upcoming suction-cup climb of the Eiffel Tower.

I had read in one of the morning papers the announcement for the upcoming marriage between Piggy and the Vicomte de Chagny. I just knew this was going to make Deadly pitch a fit.

I rode my unicycle to the Opera, left it with the valet, and entered ready for pretty much anything.

Piggy Daaé's abduction from the stage surprised everybody but me. I had no doubt that she had been smuggled away by Deadly. And I thought for sure that this was curtains for her and maybe even for "the lot of us."

I had no choice that night but to sneak into the carnival through the third cellar. Hopefully Deadly would be preoccupied with his captive. But in case he wasn't, I thought I'd better find an accomplice, someone who'd have my back. And it seemed that no one cared more about seeing Piggy freed from Deadly's clutches than Kermit.

I sent Quongo for my Suitcase of Questionable Fashions and cornered the viscount, who jumped at my proposal. The way he trusted me right away was touching—it reminded me of my old trapeze partner when I asked her to do the infamous "greased-up death-catch over Victoria Falls" routine. Hopefully this time wouldn't end like that one. (Probably not, since frogs are a lot more agile than manatees.)

So: Fast-forward through the discovery of the sleeping Chip and the surprise appearance of Animal and his s'mores-crazed tickle-footed rats, and there Kermit and I finally were in the third cellar. I shifted the stone to open the secret door, and we jumped into Deadly's haunt.

Constructing the carnival would have been surprisingly easy: Deadly was one of the chief contractors under Howard Tubman, the boorish architect of the Opera House (well, to be fair, he was an actual boar). Tubman, a member of France's oldest and fleshiest four-footed families, had been impressed with the innovative delights Deadly had built for fairs around the world and wanted him to bring that sort of inspired theatricality to the Opera House. When Deadly saw the enormous cellars, he decided to create a dwelling unknown to the rest of the Earth, where he could hide from all eyes for all time. Besides, was he not as frightening as ever?

Long after the others had stopped working, Deadly continued by himself. Without a boss to keep watch, he was free to let his dark imagination go wild. Deep underground he made all sorts of unhinged variations on those classic midway designs and came up with new inventions, too.

Of these, the most curious, horrible, and dangerous was his twist on the so-called Palace of Illusion. I knew of it from the previous version he made for the famous fun house in Bavaria. As the warning sign posted at the entryway said: "Inside you will encounter a series of endless passages lined entirely with mirrors. The mirrors create an infinity of duplicated reflections and cause disorientation, confusion, and anguished second-guessing about whether those jeans make you look fat."

Visitors who entered could only eventually escape when they pressed a nearly-impossible-to-find square of glass about the size of a piece of Bubble Yum that opened a disguised exit door in one of the reflecting panels.

So I was alarmed, to say the least, when I saw that Kermit and I had unwittingly dropped into a perilous position: We found ourselves deep inside a new and no doubt even-more-dastardly update to the Palace of Illusion.

And this one, I came to learn, was called Uncle Deadly's Maddening Mirror Maze™.

Chapter XXII

SMACK-DAB IN THE MIDDLE OF UNCLE DEADLY'S MADDENING MIRROR MAZE™

Gonzo's Journal, continued

I grabbed Kermit's arm. (It felt like a flexi straw. That guy was seriously svelte.) I worried that he wouldn't be able to stop himself from shouting to his lady friend, wherever she may be, so I clamped a hand over his mouth.

Just then, we heard a faint oink in the next room. I clutched Kermit's arm tighter so he'd stay silent, and then we distinctly heard a voice from somewhere nearby: "You must make your choice, Piggy! We either say 'I do,' or we say 'adieu'—for *good*. My 'Storm Cloud Connection' is finally finished, and now I just want to get married and do all the stuff normal folks do: build a secret bunker in the suburbs, get a neck tattoo, raise a pet bison. Why are you cringing? It doesn't have to be a bison—it could be a jellyfish. True, they're harder to walk, but at least you don't have to carry around that bison-size pooper-scooper."

I was pretty sure that Deadly hadn't heard us in his looking-glass labyrinth, otherwise he would have started the squishing at once . . .

But I'm getting ahead of myself.

I tried to think of a way to let Piggy know we were there. She just *had* to open the hidden door for us—that was the only way we could hope to help her. It could take us days, maybe even weeks to find the hidden square of glass that would trigger the door!

Suddenly, out of the blue, something heavy dropped from above and flattened Kermit with a *thud*. "Oh boy," groaned the shape as it rolled off the flummoxed frog.

"Fozzie Bear?!" I whispered in astonishment. "What are *you* doing here?"

"I was trailing the two of you," he said, getting to his feet and adjusting the fanny pack he had strapped around his waist. "Kudos to me—I guess my stakeout skills are improving! Wow," he said, giving each of us the once-over, "what're you wearing? It looks like a thrift store threw up."

I held a finger to my lips to shush him, but it was too late—Deadly had heard! Luckily, he thought the sound was some other intruder approaching from the lake. We listened as his heavy steps moved away, then he was gone.

The Vicomte de Chagny was already calling, "Piggy! *Piggy!*"

Her faint voice replied, "I must be dreaming . . . It sounds like the little frog who rescued my Jet Ski, my Kermie-wermie!"

"Piggy, you're not dreaming—it *is* me, your Kermie-wermie!"

"And me, your Gonzo-wonzo!"

"And me, your Fozzie-wozzie!"

"*Mon dieu,*" said Piggy, "how many of you *are* there?"

And just like that, another body fell from above, plopping right onto Fozzie's furry head.

"Oof, okay!" said the shape as it tried to find its footing.

"Well, that makes *four*!" I exclaimed. "Pepé, how did you find us?"

"I was following the inspector, doing like Encyclopedia Brown. I think that character's the bomb dot com."

Kermit peered up at the ceiling. "Um, just a thought, but maybe we should move away from this spot in case anyone else suddenly—"

But he spoke too late: First Statler came hurtling down from above, then Waldorf, both bouncing safely off Fozzie's big belly.

"Well, this is obviously proving to be the terrible idea I said it was," griped Waldorf to his partner as he dusted himself off. "We're no closer to knowing who stole the francs, and now we're . . . where are we?"

"Why is it so dim in here?" asked Statler, squinting to take in the surroundings. "And what are all these mirrors? It's like we've fallen into the world's worst department-store dressing room."

Waldorf eyeballed my outfit, then Kermit's. "Well, if that's what they're selling, it's no wonder they keep the lights off!"

"Never mind all that," I scoffed. "Piggy! We're just on the other side of the wall. With a surprising amount of company. And we're going to find a way to save you!"

Then Piggy spilled it all: She told us how Deadly had gone quite mad with love ("who can blame him?") and that he had decided to "make everyone sorry" if she didn't agree to marry him. He had given her till eleven o'clock that evening to give him a yes or no decision. Piggy added that Deadly had then uttered a phrase that she didn't quite understand: "If your answer is no, everybody will be enjoying the grand reopening of the Opera!"

Most people would think that was a pretty weird thing to say, but I should have figured it out instantly considering what I knew of Deadly's . . . how should I put it? *Explosive* temper. "Can you go and make sure he's left the fun house?" I asked her.

"No, because he hog-tied me!"

When we heard this, Kermit couldn't hold back—he threw propriety to the wind and cursed aloud: "*Sassafras!*" (Turns out Kermit was a pretty PG guy.)

Now our safety, the safety of all *seven* of us, depended on Piggy getting loose.

"But where *are* you, anyway?" asked Piggy. "There are only two ways in and out of this joint: One is through the Barrel of Laughs—"

Pepé interrupted. "What ees a Barrel of Laughs?"

Waldorf cracked, "One thing Fozzie will never be."

Statler added, "Yeah, he's got Van Gogh's ear for comedy!"

Before the bear could respond, I explained to Pepé that the Barrel of Laughs was one of the amusements Deadly had invented—a horizontal rotating cylinder that you try to walk through without falling down. It reminded me of the time I took a spin inside an industrial washing machine. (It had gone great till they added the detergent.)

Piggy chimed in, "The only other way out of the room is a regular door that I've never seen him open. He has forbidden me to use it, and says it is the most dangerous of the doors, the door that leads to certain peril."

"That's where *we* are, behind the most dangerous door," I told her. "We are in Uncle Deadly's Maddening Mirror Maze™!"

"Aha! So *that's* where the scoundrel's been hiding all the mirrors," she blurted.

"You've got to get to the door, Piggy," I told her. "We're trapped in miles of mirrors with no idea where the way out could be!"

"The door is bolted, but I bet I know where the key is. His hurdy-gurdy is on a stand in the corner. He told me never to touch it. I bet the key is tied to the neck or taped to the back! Oh, Kermie! Hop! Hop away! Everything is mysterious here—you are in Uncle Deadly's Maddening Mirror Maze™, I am hog-tied, and my hair is an utter disaster!"

"Piggy," said the valiant frog, "we will go from here together or perish together!"

"Hmm," said Pepé, "on that idea, I think we should actually take the group vote, okay."

"I'm never gonna give you up," Kermit continued to his love, "never gonna let you down. Never gonna run around and desert you!"[29]

From the other room we heard her exclaim, "Oh, if only I could get loose from these roller-coaster tracks!"

---

[29] Incidentally, this was the very first known instance of Rickrolling.

Pepé looked up. "Did she say 'roller coaster'?"

"There's a roller coaster down here?" said Kermit.

"Underground?" asked Statler.

"Inside a fun house?" marveled Waldorf.

Piggy answered, "You think *that's* surprising, you should get a load of the Ferris wheel."

"Ah, tied to the tracks," I recalled wistfully. "I remember one time when I chained myself to a train trestle in Transylvania—"

Kermit interrupted: "Uh, maybe reminisce later?"

"My bad. I digress."

Kermit concentrated hard for a moment, then said, "Piggy, what if you started crying? Remember that you're a great actress."

"You're darn tootin' I am! I'm a master of the Croissant Method."

"What's that?" asked Fozzie.

"I just imagine that my costar is a chocolate croissant that I can't have, and the tears flow."

"Start crying and convince Deadly that the ropes are hurting," advised Kermit, "and maybe he'll untie you!"

"Then get your hands on the key and open the door," I added. "There's strength in numbers. And, though I never in a million years would have planned it this way, there are *a lot* of us in here now. And we might as well try to take advantage of that."

Piggy shushed him: They heard heavy steps approaching through what must have been the Barrel of Laughs. Next came a tremendous sigh from Piggy, and we heard Deadly's voice: "Why are you crying, Piggy?"

"Oh, it's just that I'm in such pain, Deadly. It's the worst pain I've ever felt. These ropes are cutting off my circulation! I'm in *agony*!"

"Oh, fine then. I thought maybe I scared you."

"Oh jeez, Deadly, don't be a dunce," she said, giving up the act. "I told you that I don't find you in the least bit scary. You are 'seen and not feared,' just like you always wanted, got that? So untie me already. We made a deal. Didn't we agree that I have till eleven o'clock tonight?"

Deadly relented: "Very well, then." The footsteps dragged along the floor again. We heard some rustling. "You're free now."

"Besides, considering all those food stalls out there on the midway, there's nowhere I'd rather be than in your carnival! I haven't even tried the fried Jell-O yet."

"I suppose you make a good point. Everyone should try that before they die." And then the voice, transformed, distinctly grated out these metallic syllables: *"What the dickens are you doing with my hurdy-gurdy?!"*

Chapter XXIII

PIGGY'S METHOD TO FIGHT MADNESS

Gonzo's Journal, continued

"**I** said," the captor repeated slowly, "what are you doing with my hurdy-gurdy?!"

"I was only admiring the fine craftsmanship," Piggy insisted, trying to cover.

"Liar, liar, pants on fire!"

"Technically these are culottes." She paused to consider her course. "I just wanted to . . . look at the next room, which I've never seen and which you've always kept from me. Unlock the door, Deadly. It's a woman's curiosity," she added, attempting a coquettish tone.

"Curiosity killed the cat. Trust me," he said, drawing out each word, "you don't want to find out what it could do to the pig. Now, give me back my hurdy-gurdy!"

Piggy shouted, "Hey!" as he evidently snatched the instrument from her hands. At that moment, the viscount could not help uttering a *ribbit* of rage.

"What was that?" said Deadly, instantly amused. "Did you hear something, Piggy?"

"Nope, no, uh-uh, not a thing."

"I thought I heard . . . a *ribbit*."

"A ribbit! Are you tripping, Deadly? That was me, because you surprised me when you grabbed the hurdy-gurdy, you big blue brute."

"Really?"

"How could you doubt me?" she replied, trying to work up some tears.

"I think you're fibbing again."

"It's not fibbing, it's the *Croissant Method*!"

"Ah, I understand now—there is a frog in Uncle Deadly's Maddening Mirror Maze™. The frog you want to tie the knot with, perhaps?"

"That's crazy talk! I just got out of *your* knots, why would I want to go into *his*?"

Another nasty chuckle. "Well, it won't take long to find out, Piggy, my love. We don't even have to unlock the door to see what's happening in Uncle Deadly's Maddening Mirror Maze™. We only need to go up those stairs and draw back the black curtain that covers the one-way mirror right up there, near the ceiling. We just need to put out the light in here."

Then we heard Piggy lay it on thick again, trying to

distract him: "No, don't turn out the light! Didn't you know that I'm afraid of the dark? I'm sooooo frightened! I don't care about that room anymore. I was curious before, but you've told me what it is now, so my curiosity is satisfied—end of movie, credits done, popcorn bucket thrown on the floor! . . . Oh dear, it is quite dark now, isn't it?"

And he must have flicked a second switch, because the hallways in the maze were instantly alive with lights of every kind—multicolored, flashing, clusters of laser pinpoints—all multiplied to infinity by the mirrored walls. It was like the dance floor at my cousin Chaim's bar mitzvah, but without all the kids on Snapchat.

"Am I having a seizure?" said Waldorf, looking around.

"No, I think we're in one of those nightclubs," Statler replied.

Waldorf scoffed. "You think a bouncer would ever let us in? The only place we're VIPs is the AARP."

I noticed that Deadly's disco-light torture had started to take hold of Fozzie, who kept trying to escape but only succeeded in knocking his head against mirror after mirror, never progressing more than a few feet.

"How did I get myself into this situation?" fretted Fozzie. "I should have never become a cop. I wasn't even good at my *first* job, as a night watchman. In just one month, someone stole three nights!"

In the next room I heard Deadly say to Piggy, "Go on—ascend the steps to peer into Uncle Deadly's Maddening Mirror Maze™. See what lies inside."

We heard her steps, then her head came into view. Wow, she wasn't kidding: Her hair *was* a mess. She gave a little, almost-imperceptible wave to Kermit and blurted, *"Mon chéri!"*

Deadly thought she was talking to him. He melted a bit. "Oh, Piggy, what did you say?"

"I was saying, 'Just as I thought: There's no one there, *mon chéri.*' I definitely didn't wave at anyone. Definitely not at *six* anyones, and especially not two of them dressed in the worst outfits I have maybe ever seen. Not a single soul in there committing full-on fashion faux pas, that's for certain."

"Well, that's lucky, since fashion faux pas are my kryptonite."

One of her impeccably shaped eyebrows rose. "Ohhhhhh, really?"

I already knew this, of course, but what good were our bad outfits for defeating Deadly if we could never be face-to-face with him?

We heard the creature soften and say, "Oh, *ma chérie,*

couldn't we make a go of it? If one wishes, one can get used to everything. Except gluten-free bread."

"Look, U.D., all due respect, but I don't think we really have a lot in common outside the opera."

"Oh, but you would have lots of fun with me. I know card tricks, and magic, and mime. Look! I'm trapped in an invisible box!"

"Oooh," said Piggy, sounding genuinely impressed, "that is *très* realistic."

"Plus, I am the greatest ventriloquist that ever lived. Oh, but you're laughing! I love your laugh. Perhaps you don't believe that I'm that good? Listen." We could hear him quite clearly as he said, "Here, I raise my mask a little, only a little! You see my lips? They're not moving! My mouth is closed and yet you hear my voice."

"Uh, *yeah*," said Piggy with a roll of her eyes, "that's generally how ventriloquism works."

"Where should I throw my voice? In your left ear? In your right ear?"

"Hey, cool—stereo!"

"Maybe into the Barrel of Laughs? Into those two little Tupperware bowls on the shelf? Listen, dear, it's Deadly's voice in the little bowl on the right: What does it say? *'Shall I choose the sweet?'* And now, snap! What does it say in the little bowl on the left? *'Shall I choose the salty?'* And now, snap! Here's Deadly in the hurdy-gurdy. And now, snap! Here's Deadly talking through Yolanda onstage, saying, 'It's I, Mr. Cow! *Mooooo! Mooooo!'*"

"It was *you*!" she exclaimed. "You did the mooing that ruined Yolanda! Oh, *snap*!"

"And now," he continued, a little manic, "here's Deadly talkin' loud, here's Deadly doin' fine. Deadly's goin' strong, Deadly's all alone . . . Deadly's lettin' go. *Deadly?!*" He paused—it sounded almost like he sobbed once, then recovered. "Listen, Piggy, my dear! Listen! There's Deadly now behind the door of Uncle Deadly's Maddening Mirror Maze™!"

Oh, the ventriloquist's relentless voice! It seemed to be *everywhere*. It passed through the little invisible window, along the walls. It ran around us, between us. On he went: "Why did I do it, huh? What did it get me? I had a dream! I dreamed it for you, Piggy!"

It was as if Deadly was *right there*, in the mirrored halls with us, having his almost-eleven-o'clock number! It felt so real, I thought I could grab him. But, already, quicker than an echo, his voice had leaped back behind the wall.

"Oh, Deadly!" said Piggy. "You wear me out with your vocal tricks and Sondheim references. Don't go on! And my goodness, isn't it getting toasty in here? I'm hotter than a polar bear in a steam room. We should open that door to let in some air!"

"Oh yes," replied Deadly's voice in a flat, menacing tone, "there's an idea. Why *don't* we open a door."

A moment later we watched as a nearby panel in one of the mirrored walls swung open.

"I meant *this* door," we heard Piggy say, pounding with her fists and sounding a little alarmed, "the one that leads from this room to the maze. It's still closed!"

"Oh, I know what you meant," Deadly shot back with an icy edge in his voice.

We all exchanged glances—what were we going to find through that open door? Where did it lead?

"I don't know, guys," I whispered. "It could be a trap."

Kermit was determined: "But it might be the way to Piggy!"

"A wise man once say," began Pepé, "'Twenty years from now joo will be more disappointed by the things that joo didn't do than by the ones joo did do.'"

"That's the spirit," said Kermit.

"It would maybe be better, okay, if the day after he say it, he didn't forgot to tie the other end of his bungee to the bridge."

Waldorf said, "If only we had a weapon!"

Fozzie pulled a rubber chicken out of his fanny pack.

"Hey! Would this help?"

"And what exactly," asked Statler, "is that?"

"It's my Patronus. Wocka wocka!" Fozzie reached into the fanny pack again and found something else. "Oh, I forgot that I also have this whoopee cushion."

"If pooting was really the solution," said Waldorf dismissively, "Statler would have had us out of here long ago."

Kermit shushed them. "Guys! Come on! I know we're all a little frustrated and confused—"

"And scared," added Fozzie.

"And gassy," said Statler.

"But we've got to pull together," Kermit implored. "Piggy needs us."

"The frog ees right, okay."

"Now," concluded Kermit, "let's save the day, or die trying!"

The others charged ahead into the next room. They didn't suspect as I did that what was ahead of us was almost certainly worse than what we were leaving behind.

Chapter XXIV

PRISONERS BY THE POUND

Gonzo's Journal, continued

Carrying my little lantern, I followed the gang into the next room, which turned out to be round like a circus tent and about the size of a small school gymnasium.

The good news? Not a mirror in sight.

The bad news? No windows and no doors, except for the one that we just—

But drat! It was already gone: The panel we came through had closed and seamlessly blended into the wall.

We took a look around. The walls were smooth and solid wood, so scaling them was out of the question. I couldn't quite make out how high the ceiling was in the low light. The glow of the lantern didn't reach.

Kermit said, "What if we all climb up on each other's shoulders?"

Waldorf shook his head. "I can barely climb out of a bed."

But it was clear that even if Kermit, Fozzie, Pepé, and I all stacked ourselves chicken-fight style, we still couldn't get near enough to the ceiling, wherever it was up there.

Meanwhile, the inspector was walking about like a lunatic, mindlessly zipping and unzipping his fanny pack. "Sorry, guys," he said, his eyes a little wild, "but I should let you know that when I get nervous, I start talking in riddles. Like: If a red house is made of red bricks, a yellow house is made of yellow bricks, and a pink house is made of pink bricks, what is a green house made of?"

Kermit said, "Is it best if we just don't pay attention to you?"

Pepé overrode the frog. "But okay, what *ees* a green house made of?"

"Glass," exclaimed Fozzie, flashing jazz hands at them. "Also, you know what kind of room has no door and no windows? A mushroom! Oh boy," he said, shaking his head. "Sorry, it's a joke reflex. I can't stop!"

"All right, Fozzie, we don't have time for any funny business," I warned him.

Statler rolled his eyes. "His funny business went bankrupt long ago."

I kept hunting for a weak point in the wall to press, just like Deadly's other pivot systems. I hunted and hunted, feeling as high as my hands could go. Deadly was about the same height as me, and I thought that he wouldn't have put the spring beyond where he could reach.

Now the bear had begun to babble. "What comes once in a minute, twice in a moment, but never once in a thousand years? The letter *M*!"

Waldorf shook his head and said, "I'd give that one an *F*."

Meanwhile, I found nothing, absolutely nothing. We were totally stuck in this round room, no compass, no guide or anything. And we heard not a peep from Piggy. Oh, I couldn't imagine what danger awaited us if she couldn't help or if I didn't locate that spring! But, as hard as I searched, I found zilch. Still . . . if I could somehow lure Deadly into the room, our outfits might overpower him. It was worth a try.

I called out, "Yo, Deadly! I saved your life once, and I'm calling in the favor now. Deadly?" I paused, listening. "You finally have Piggy—what more do you need?"

We heard his voice from beyond the wall. "You have a point, Gonzo. Maybe I do owe you. In all the time I've known you, you've never deceived me. And as much as I hate to admit it, I feel a soft spot for your fuzzy face."

From across the room, a door appeared in the wall, and in Deadly walked, just a few feet. "I'm prepared to let bygones be—" But he froze in place and drew a hand to his eyes, covering them. "What the devil are you *wearing*?!"

"It's only a fanny pack," said Fozzie, chagrined.

"Gonzo, you badly dressed double-crosser! And the frog, too?" He was peeking through his gnarled fingers. "Are those clamdiggers *argyle*?! Horrors! I should have known not to trust you!"

"Guys! Rush the door!" I yelled, but no one was quick enough, and before we could reach it, Deadly had retreated and closed the panel solidly behind him.

From behind the wall he barked bitterly, "How dare you try to disarm me with your terrible wardrobe. You have betrayed me, Gonzo, and you will pay dearly. Let the walloping begin!"

Just then, I heard the whine of what sounded like a machine starting up, a *big* one—its mechanized rumble shook the floor. Then something massive descended in a blink from the darkness above us, slamming to the ground, very nearly turning Pepé into a prawn pancake! It lifted back up into the darkness and a few seconds later it came down again, and this time I caught a glimpse of what we were facing: a huge padded mallet the size of an oil drum, on some sort of metal arm, connecting with the floor again and again, pounding in a random pattern, shaking the ground beneath our feet each time.

It hit the space between Statler and Waldorf with a BANG.

It hit right next to Kermit with a BOOM.

It hit just behind Fozzie with a CRASH.

I realized what we were now facing. It was Deadly's other universally loved carnival invention: We were inside an oversize Whac-A-Mole game! But in this version *we* were the moles, and we had no holes to hide in! We all scurried about, trying to avoid getting clobbered.

It was now obvious to me that this was how Beauregard had met his end.

He hadn't been bright, but he had been a hard worker. He cleaned so thoroughly that he would have even tackled the cellars where few went. Deadly no doubt found his presence annoying because he couldn't come and go as he pleased. I suspect that the janitor had accidentally activated the secret stone while washing the walls, and that led to him falling into the maze and becoming a victim of Deadly's eventual Whac job.

Were we to be squished as Beauregard had been?

We continued scrambling to and fro to avoid taking a pounding. Pepé grabbed Statler and Waldorf in his four arms and tried his best to hustle them out of the way of the crushing blows. (As for me, I couldn't resist deliberately taking a few direct hits just for fun.)

Kermit cried out, "How can we stop this infernal machine?!"

Fozzie frantically unzipped his fanny pack and again pulled out the rubber chicken and whoopee cushion. Helplessly, he threw both at the massive mallet as it smacked the floor. The chicken went wide, but the cushion landed right beneath the lowering hammer, which pressed out a robust *fuuuuuuuuuuuurrrrrrt*.

Fozzie's moves may have been futile, but they sparked an idea. I reached into my pocket and was relieved to discover it was still there: the banana peel! I pulled it out. Maybe, just maybe . . .

"Hey, riddle guy," I said to Fozzie, feeling cocky as I held the peel in my right hand and wound up for a pitch. "If a crocodile makes shoes, what does a banana make?"

The bear looked up expectantly. "I don't know, Gonzo—what does a banana make?"

"Slippers!" And I threw the peel exactly where I wanted it to land: right under the mallet as it connected with the ground. Just as I hoped, it skidded off the fruit skin and wrenched to the side, bending its steel arm and bringing the whole contraption to a jolting, screeching, earsplitting halt. The device trembled briefly with one last tremor of life, then that was it.

The ordeal was over.

Slapstick had saved the day.

"Yayyyyyyyyyy!" rejoiced Kermit, arms waving above his head triumphantly.

We all fell to the floor, totally pooped.

Lying on my back, I let my head loll to the left and happened to see something I couldn't have spied while standing up. I dragged myself closer, and there, in a groove in the floor, was the black head of a nail. But all the other nails around it were silver. At last I had discovered the spring! I felt the nail and pinched it between two fingers . . . I lifted it . . . And then . . .

It didn't open a door in the wall as I had hoped it would, but instead it opened a nearby trapdoor in the floor about an inch. I folded back the lid and reached down into the darkness, feeling around. There was a stone, then another . . . it was a staircase to another cellar. I worried it was another of Deadly's tricks, but without any other options, I grabbed my lantern, which had miraculously survived the whacking, and down I went. Everyone followed.

The staircase led into total darkness. We soon reached the bottom. It felt damp in there—I figured the lake must be on the other side of the wall. Though the lantern's candle was low, we could now distinguish shapes around us . . . boxy shapes . . . Crates?

There were quite a lot of them. Maybe there was something inside that we could use to break out of the room above us. After half lifting one to make sure it was full, Kermit and I dropped to our knees and, working together, pried open the lid.

"What's this?" asked Kermit. The viscount reached in. I stooped to look, holding my lantern over the open top . . . and instantly threw away the light so hard that it broke.

"Oh, please do not tell me that joo saw a cricket, okay!" squeaked Pepé, recoiling.

What I had seen in Kermit's hands was not a cricket. It was *fireworks*!

Chapter XXV

THE SWEET OR THE SALTY:
WHICH WILL IT BE?

Gonzo's Journal, concluded

The discovery of the cellar full of fireworks finally explained what Uncle Deadly had meant when he said to Piggy, "Yes or no? If your answer is no, everybody will celebrate the Opera's grand reopening!" He meant the building would have a hole right through the center of it, because the combined power of these fireworks would practically launch the Paris Opera House into orbit like a giant space shuttle! Which is a thing that will be invented in 1981!

Deadly had given her until eleven o'clock that night. He'd chosen that time perfectly: There would be a full house up there in the fancy-pants theater, the finest shoulders in the world decked with the richest jewels. At eleven o'clock, if Piggy said no, we might all be treated to a very up-close-and-personal fireworks display that'd make Crazy Harry's extravaganzas seem puny!

What else could Piggy say but no? She was sweet on Kermit, and she was no pushover, even when facing down a big blue bully. But she didn't understand that her choice could have very dangerous consequences beyond just her Facebook relationship status.

From the cellar, we made our way up the stone steps and through the trapdoor, back into the round room. I said to the group with a gulp, "We're standing right over the crates of spinners and sparklers and rockets—"

"And crickets," added petrified Pepé.

But I barely heard him, because a terrible thought hit me. "What time is it, anyway? Eleven o'clock might already be *right now*!"

Everyone panicked. I shouted, they shouted: I called out to Deadly, Kermit called out to Piggy, Fozzie called out to his rubber chicken. And the seconds were ticking by.

"Doesn't anyone have a watch?" I asked. (A daredevil's wrist is not a good place to strap on glass.)

Just then a glow lit up the immediate area, and Pepé said, "It's ten fifty-five, okay." He held up his smartphone.

"You have a *phone*?!" Fozzie yelped. "Call nine-one-one already!"

"Come on—do joo really think I get a signal down here?" Pepé showed him the phone's face. "I have AT&T!"

Suddenly we heard footsteps in the next room, then Piggy said, "Kermit! Everyone!" We were now all talking at once, on either side of the wall.

Piggy was so relieved. She wasn't sure that she would find us alive. Her captor had been terrible, she said. He'd done nothing but rave, waiting for her to give him the answer that she refused to give. "He left and said, 'You have just five minutes more to ponder the sweet and the salty! Choose correctly or be sorry!'"

"Cool! A riddle!" said Fozzie, perking up.

"He told me to look inside the two Tupperware bowls on the table. One's filled with chocolate truffles, the other with nacho cheese corn chips. He says the one I pick is going to give him my answer. If I eat the sweet, that means I'm saying yes. If I choose the salty, that means no. But I think there's a trick involved, because his last words as he left were, 'The sweets, my sweet! Be careful of the sweets! They just might be a flavor explosion!'"

"It seems to me that if you eat the sweets," I told her, "not only will your taste buds explode, but so will the building! Considering how much Deadly loves his clever mechanisms, I'm pretty sure that the bowls are weighted, and as you eat from one, it will get lighter, tipping the scale to set off an electric current that ignites the fireworks' fuses!"

Kermit was considering. "Did Deadly give any hints about the salty?"

"Yes," she said. "Something like, 'If you eat the salty, there may be a rain of tears,' and something about 'soaking and drowning' . . ."

Soaked and drowned? What the devil did *that* mean? Perhaps it was the *salty* that would blow everything up. Surely, if Piggy perished, his tears would flow, right? I shared the thought, and we all started talking, some of us telling Piggy to avoid the sweets, others advising that she skip the salty, all of us giving our various reasons for thinking as we did.

"Well," said Piggy, finally cutting us off and clearly exasperated, "this little chat has been wildly helpful. Uh-oh, here he comes!"

We heard his steps passing through the Barrel of Laughs, and I hollered, "Deadly!"

With extraordinary calmness, he replied coldly: "Well, well—you're still alive, Gonzo. Now your fate rests on the choice of the fair Miss Piggy. She has not touched the sweets"—he spoke so deliberately!—"and she has not touched the salty"—so composed!—"but it is not too late for her to do the right thing. Look at the snacks."

"You know how pigs can't resist truffles," said Piggy anxiously, clearly tempted.

"Or you could have the deliciously zesty cheese corn chips—"

"Powdered cheese is the *best* cheese!"

After a long, agonizing moment, we heard Piggy gobbling. She said decisively, "There! I have eaten the chips . . ."

Oh, the anxiety we felt in the Whac-A-Mole room! Waiting! Waiting to find ourselves blown to bits!

Piggy continued, "And now I'm gonna tackle those truffles!"

"No!" yelled Deadly. "Stop! You can't have *both*! And, well, you *did* have both!"

"I couldn't help it," she said with her mouth full. "That was too much pressure, and everyone knows I'm a stress eater!"

I felt something crack beneath our feet, then a curious hissing sound came through the open trapdoor. Was it the fuses of a hundred rockets being lit?

"Noooo," moaned Deadly, "eating *both* was not an option! My contraption can't operate if you do that. You've broken it!"

The hiss grew in volume, but it wasn't the sound of fire. It was more like the hiss of . . . water? And now it became a gurgling sound. *Guggle! Guggle!*

I rushed to the trapdoor and descended a few stairs.

We could hear the lake water seeping up in between the stones in the floor and dribbling down the walls. It lapped at the bottoms of the crates.

We were saved!

The water rose in the cellar, above the crates, filling them and drenching the gunpowder inside the rockets and Roman candles. And we went up the stairs again, step by step, with the water following us.

Hmm. I started to think this was maybe not 100 percent a good thing.

The water soon bubbled up out of the cellar and spread along the Whac-A-Mole floor, which quickly became a little pond that our feet were splashing through. If this went on, the whole fun house on the lake, if not the whole carnival and the cellar that contained it, would be submerged.

"Deadly! Turn off the tap!"

But Deadly didn't reply to me. We heard nothing but the water—it was already halfway to our waists! We were all alone, in the dark, with the cold water that kept rising!

By this time, we had lost our footholds and were spinning around, carried away by an irresistible whirlpool that spun us and dashed us against the dark walls. Had we survived getting squished like Beauregard only to be drowned like waterlogged moles?

We whirled around like so much wreckage. And the water rose still higher. Even the good swimmers among us were losing their strength, trying to grab something, *anything* on the walls. But there was nothing under our groping fingers. We whirled around again in the circular current. The water had almost reached the ceiling of the room, and we began to sink.

One last effort!

Our last cries: "Deadly! Piggy!"

Guggle, guggle in our ears. *Guggle, guggle* at the bottom of the dark water. And, before losing consciousness entirely, I seemed to hear, between two last *guggles*:

> *"You can check out any time you like,*
> *but you can never leave!"*

Chapter XXVI

THE PHANTOM'S TUMULTUOUS TAIL
COMES TO ITS END

The previous chapter marks the conclusion of the Great Gonzo's written narrative. He, Monsieur Kermit de Chagny, and their companions did, in fact, survive, thanks to a moment of selfless sacrifice by Piggy Daaé. And I had their side of the story from the lips of Gonzo himself.

When I went to see him one morning, he was living in a little flat on the bank of the river Seine. He had courted Camilla, the dainty dancer from the Opera's *corps de poulet*, and the two had married. She'd made her husband promise not to talk about the terrible events of the fifth cellar, but I, as an historian pledged to the truth, had convinced him that it was important to preserve the record faithfully.

His simian servant, Quongo, showed me in. Gonzo, with his sizable eyes and that one-of-a-kind honker, stood near a window overlooking a garden where Camilla was hunting and pecking for her breakfast. He told me his story with perfect lucidity.

Here we step back in time, to the day of the watery onslaught.

When Gonzo awakened after the flooding of the Whac-A-Mole room, he found himself lying comfortably . . . in a ball pit. Around him he could see Kermit, Fozzie, Pepé, and the two old fogies, all sleeping atop hundreds of multicolored balls about the size of grapefruits. He deduced correctly that they were still in the fun house.

Standing over them was the figure of the creature, now in a Batman mask. He bent down over Gonzo and said, "Holy close call." Gonzo noticed Piggy Daaé sitting on the edge of the pit, keeping watch and polishing off the bag of nacho cheese chips.

"You are now saved, all six of you," said Deadly. "But the waters are still rising, and they will not stop till they fill this cellar. Soon I shall take you up to the surface of the earth, as she has implored me to do."

Thereupon he rose, without any further explanation, and disappeared into the other room.

Gonzo heard the hurdy-gurdy as Deadly began to play his masterwork, "The Storm Cloud Connection." But it was now transformed—the dark intensity had given way to sweetness and light, with only a soupçon of wistfulness, and the chords had shifted from minor to major. The lyrics were completely changed. The metaphor of the storm was gone, replaced by the beauty that emerges in its aftermath. The song—incredibly!—was now a testament to optimism. Deadly sang of discovering a "rainbow connection" that united lovers, dreamers, and even the creature himself.

But exhausted Gonzo heard no more, as he quickly fell back to sleep and did not wake again until he was in his own room at home. Quongo nourished him with mashed bananas and told him that the night before, he found his boss propped against the door of their flat, where he had been brought by a stranger who had rung the bell, then fled.

The next morning, after Gonzo had quickly fired off concerned notes to each of his companions in the ordeal to inquire about their health, Quongo announced the arrival of someone who refused to give his name, who wore a hooded cloak to hide his face, and who declared simply that he did not intend to leave until he had spoken with the master of the house.

Gonzo at once figured out who his singular visitor was and asked him to be shown in. His hunch was right: It was the ghost—it was Uncle Deadly!

Gonzo rose to his feet as Deadly entered, demanding, "Is everyone all right? Where are Kermit de Chagny and Piggy Daaé—are they alive or dead?!"

"I will tell you everything, I promise," uttered Deadly. "But first you must know the event that changed me, that took me from storm clouds to rainbows."

Gonzo was wildly curious, so he consented. Quongo entered and placed plates of banana crème pie before them, then settled protectively on a pouf in the corner not too far from his employer.

Deadly took a deep breath and began: "The fun house was flooding. The water was finding its way into all the rooms and beyond, throughout the carnival, rising slowly but certainly. Piggy was tending to Kermit. And as much as I didn't want to see it, I could not deny the genuine love she had for him. I was struck by its purity. Then and there, I experienced an epiphany: They clearly deserved to be together. A life with Piggy by my side was not to be, and I was surprised to realize that I no longer mourned that fact. No, Gonzo, Piggy is not dead! She is a good, honest pig, and she saved your life at a moment when I would not have given a tuppence for your hairy hide. Or for any of you!"

He sat down on a chair. "You had all ceased to exist for me, I tell you, and you were going to perish with the others! Only, mark me, when you were all yelling like the devil because of the water, Piggy came to me with her beautiful blue eyes wide open and swore to me that she didn't fear me at all. It was not the first time anyone told me that, thinking I wanted to hear it. But it was the first time I actually *believed* anyone who said it. Still the water rose, and I had to get everyone out. Six souls! Piggy beseeched me to take you all up to the surface of the earth. And, at last, I cleared the fun house of you all—all except the frog . . ."

"And just what have you done with the Vicomte de Chagny?" interjected Gonzo.

"Ah, I intended to hold him hostage. But in one profound action, my world was altered." Deadly rose solemnly and, overcome by emotion, began to tremble a bit: "I . . . stepped up to Piggy, more timid than a little child, and she did not run away. No, she stayed. And . . . I . . . kissed her!"

Gonzo winced involuntarily. "Gross—"

"—on her forehead—"

"—okay, that's less gross, sorry—"

"—and she did not draw back her pink skin from my

285

blue lips! You have your chicken ballerina, your Camilla. You can't know how it felt for me! My happiness was so great, I cried. I fell at Piggy's feet, and I kissed her Manolo Blahnik pumps."

The masked creature sobbed aloud, and Gonzo himself could not retain his tears. Even Quongo was blubbering. "My tears flowed until I couldn't see her, so I tore off my mask, the plain, form-fitted white one that covered every inch of my monstrous face. And Piggy did not flee! She stayed! I looked at the mask in my hands, one of the many infernal shields I had hidden behind for most of my life. This emblem of my shame. And in one impulsive moment, I brought it violently down upon my knee, breaking it—the mask, not my knee."

Just then, Deadly's hood slipped back off his head to reveal the broken mask in question, now only covering the right side of his face from his forehead down along his nose to the cheekbone. Gonzo noted, "It's very striking—iconic, even. It would look good on a show poster, or maybe a book jacket. But I thought you said you didn't need it anymore."

"Baby steps."

Gonzo pressed, "But what of Kermit? And what about Constantine and Janice, who haven't been seen since that fateful night his coach dashed across town?

Have you imprisoned them, as well?"

"Goodness, no! They eloped and are en route to upstate New York. I hear they're going to settle in Janice's hometown, a magical place called Woodstock."

"Well, that is a relief," Gonzo said with a sigh.

"They found their happiness, and I wanted the same for Piggy and Kermit. Yesterday in the cellar I held in my hand a ring, *the* ring: the Ring Pop that she had lost and that I found again in a dark corner of the Opera near the costume shop. I dusted it off and slipped it onto her big little finger and said, 'There! Take it! This shall be my wedding present . . . for you and your beloved frog!' I brought them to the midway, put them on the Tunnel of Love, and explained how the ride ended at another secret exit from the cellar. I asked Piggy to come back one night soon when I was dead. I told her she would learn of the event from an ad I would put in the *Revue Théâtrale.* I asked her to cross the lake in the greatest secrecy with the ring, which I requested that she wear until that moment. . . . I told her where she would find my body. And she swore that she would . . ."

"But you look fine to me," said Gonzo. "How could you be dying? That doesn't seem possible."

Just then Camilla entered and, upon seeing Deadly, blurted out a terrified *"Bgark!"*

Her blue-nosed husband pulled her close.

Embarrassed, Deadly quickly put his hood back on, covering his face, and collected himself to depart. He told Gonzo, "We shall not see each other again. I leave you with my gratitude for your kindnesses and my deep apology for squishing Beauregard and Beaker."

Gonzo asked no more questions. He escorted Deadly to the door of his flat, and Quongo got him a cab. Gonzo heard the masked creature say to the one-clawed driver: "To the Opera. And step on it."

They had seen the blue reptile-dragon for the last time.

Three weeks later, all but a few Parisians were puzzled to read this curious notice in the *Revue Théâtrale*:

"Deadly is dead as a doornail."

Epilogue

And there you have it: the singular, utterly unvarnished, completely veracious story of the Phantom of the Opera. It is no longer possible to deny that he really lived or to assert that his motivations were evil or lacked their own justifications, however twisted they may have appeared.

There is no need to repeat here how greatly the case excited all of Paris. I repeat, there is no need to repeat that. The pignapping of the porcine singer under such exceptional conditions; the disappearance of Count Constantine and Janice Sorelli; the sugar coma of the IT guy; Yolanda's woebegone whiskers: What tragedies, what passions, what crimes had surrounded the idyll of Kermit and the charming snack fanatic Piggy!

The reader may wonder what became of that ample-figured artist and her devoted paramour. On a morning soon after the final events described herein, TMZ showed up on Kermit's doorstep to find no one home. Later, when the reporters called at Mildred Huxtetter's house to ask about Piggy's whereabouts, the good old lady just smiled mischievously and claimed that her daughter had gone on extended holiday.[30]

Mildred told the press that she *was* troubled, however, by the unexplained disappearance of her housekeeper, Lenny, who hadn't shown up for work in more than ten days. But the journalists scoffed at investigating some layperson lizard when the public was only interested in hearing about the fascinating pig and her faithful frog.

Mildred tried to contact Fozzie Bear regarding her missing housekeeper, but to no avail. The inspector had resigned, leaving law enforcement to travel the stand-up comedy circuit, and was last reported happily playing Peoria.

Long after the inspector survived the soaking in the cellars and abruptly abandoned the case of the Opera ghost, newspapers still tried to contact him, at intervals, to fathom the mystery. Even Fleet Scribbler, who knew all the gossip of the theater scene, wrote in a follow-up

---

[30] I have it on good authority that the couple was already on a Royal Caribbean Icebreaker Cruise to the North Pole. Perhaps they, like the elusive Santa, would hide themselves in arctic exile, far away from the gossipmongers—at least until the book tour commenced for Piggy's tell-all autobiography, *#Blessed*.

column: "We recognize the touch of the Phantom of the Opera in all this brouhaha." And that was expressed by way of irony. The whole affair was still just a diversion, only half believed by most.

Yet there were undeniable proofs in both the relics archived by the Phantom and from the recollections of Gonzo. It fell to my lot to complete and preserve everything regarding the singular building and its most remarkable secret recesses.

And I have particularly unique insight into some of the episodes.

For instance, when superstitious Grosse first heard a mysterious voice in Box Five, he believed himself cursed; and then, when the voice began to ask for money, he deduced that he was being victimized by a shrewd blackmailer. Already tired of his job for a number of reasons, he went away without trying to investigate further into the motives of that curious spook who had forced such a unique set of requirements upon him. He bequeathed the whole mystery to his successors and heaved a sigh of relief when he was rid of a business that had endlessly challenged him without amusing him in the least.

Readers can find some key explanations in the parts of Statler's memoir that he devotes to the ghost. I quote these lines, which are particularly interesting because they describe the very simple manner in which the famous case of the purloined francs was closed. Wrote Statler:

As for the Phantom, he sure pulled off a doozy, then he impressed me even more with one final twist.

Like all good pranksters, he knew when a joke had gone too far. Because after that useless Fozzie Bear entered the picture following Piggy Daaé's disappearance, we discovered, on Waldorf's chair, an envelope that bore the words (in red ink, of course) "With the Phantom's compliments." It contained all the money that he'd succeeded in slyly, oh-so-patiently swiping from us for sport, plus—in a touch that we couldn't help but applaud—a Starbucks gift card.

Waldorf and I agreed right then and there to make the Phantom an honorary Delta Lotta Pranks fraternity member. So wherever you may be, we raise our Pumpkin Spice Lattes to you, brother!

Like Statler's memoirs, all the documents relating to the existence of the Phantom have been checked and confirmed by a number of important discoveries of which I am justly proud. They include Gonzo's manuscript; Piggy Daaé's letters; and the extensive statements made by Pepé, Rizzo, Scooter, and Sam Eagle, as well as by

Camilla, Johnny Fiama,[31] and Janice Sorelli.[32]

If the reader will visit the Opera one morning and sneak away from the tour guide to go where she pleases, let her go to Box Five and knock on the enormous column that separates it from the next box. She will find that the column sounds hollow, because indeed it is.

After that, do not be astonished by the suggestion that it was occupied by the voice of the ghost: There is room enough inside the column for *two* blue reptile-dragons.[33] If you are surprised that when the various incidents occurred, no one turned around to look at the column, you must remember that it has the appearance of solid marble, and that the voice contained in it seemed like it came from the *opposite* side, for, as we have seen, the Phantom was an unsurpassed ventriloquist.

The column was elaborately carved and decorated with the sculptor's chisel; and I do believe that one day someone very keen will discover the panel that could be raised or lowered at will to allow the ghost's mysterious

[31] The worthy Mama Fiama, I am sorry to say, has since passed on to the great Olive Garden in the sky.

[32] Enterprising Janice retired from dance and carved out a second career for herself, eventually starting her own holistic lifestyle website, Patchouli.

[33] Though only one of that kind ever existed. Of that fact I'm eminently qualified to be absolutely certain.

exchanges with Mama Fiama.

However, all these revelations are nothing, to my mind, compared to the one made in the managers' office: Within a couple inches of the desk chair, a secret trapdoor was discovered. It is the width of a board in the flooring and the length of a forearm and no longer; it falls back silently like the lid of a hinged box, with just enough clearance for a hand to come out and dexterously reach into a pocket to exchange play money for real money, even when the envelope is Krazy Glued to the lining.

That is the way the francs went! And it is also the way by which they were honorably returned. The reader knows and guesses the rest. It is all in keeping with this incredible and yet factual story.

Oh, that Deadly—a more brilliant, cunning, and clever brain never existed, it's clear. But the poor, unhappy soul! Shall we pity him? Shall we curse him? He asked only to be "someone," like everybody else. But he was too scary, and he had to hide his genius or use it to play tricks, when, with an ordinary face, he would have been one of the most distinguished individuals on the planet! He had a heart, intellect, and talent that could have dazzled the world.

I have prayed that history might show him mercy notwithstanding his crimes. But that is perhaps unlikely. For just last month a skeleton believed to be his was discovered. It was stumbled upon when high-speed Internet cables were being installed throughout the Opera House—the Wi-Fi had always been notoriously spotty.

How did they know it was the Phantom? Credit the CSI Paris team, which was able to date the remains back to just after the flooding of the cellar.

More revealing still: The skeleton was determined to be reptilian, with a telltale tail just like Deadly's. The plastic base of a Ring Pop was also discovered on the corpse's finger, the candy having long dissolved, or perhaps having been nibbled away by a pack of rats with a sweet tooth. Investigators conferred with Fozzie Bear and concluded that it must be the selfsame piece of jewelry given by the Phantom to Mademoiselle Piggy, and which she in turn had placed on his dead finger in a gesture of loving friendship, as he had requested.[34]

But was this body accorded any noteworthy funeral services? Was it eulogized one iota? Were its contributions to the arts appreciated? No, nope, and not at all. It was unceremoniously buried in a potter's field.

No amount of searching turned up any evidence of the carnival on the lake, assuredly a consequence of Deadly

---

[34] No one questioned the morning coat and formally pleated ascot tie found on the corpse, as it seemed vaguely in keeping with the kind of attire the Phantom would wear . . .

blocking all the secret entrances as well as complete submersion following the flooding of those particular areas of the cellars. If anyone did happen to discover the secret trapdoor through which Kermit, Gonzo, Fozzie, and the rest dropped into Uncle Deadly's Maddening Mirror Maze™, they would peer down only to see pitch-black lake water almost touching the very floor under their feet.

So the search for the elusive Phantom was terminated. The authorities were satisfied, the managers relieved: The perpetrator had been identified. And the perpetrator, it appeared, had perished.

They'd all arrived at a neat and tidy solution and seemingly vanquished the darkness.[35] It was time to move on. Already, new intrigues and scandals were capturing the public's attention. And another opera season had begun.

Accordingly, a talented young singer, Lydia the Pig, recently joined the company and has created quite a hullabaloo. Indeed, she shows no small amount of promise. Now all she needs is a devoted mentor who can develop her into a diva worthy to follow in the fabled footsteps of Piggy Daaé.

And I think I know the perfect candidate for the job.

---

[35] But is darkness ever *really* vanquished? Or does it just burrow deeper—to, say, a *sixth* cellar that some industrious contractor could have covertly carved out during construction and about which no one knows? Metaphorically speaking, of course . . . Toodeloo!